LOOKING FOR THE SUN

Thank you!

Thank you!

LOOKING FOR THE SUN

S.R. CARTER

NEW DEGREE PRESS

LOOKING FOR THE SUN

ISBN   978-1-63676-824-3   *Paperback*

          978-1-63730-218-7   *Kindle Ebook*

          978-1-63730-268-2   *Ebook*

Walk into the forest until the moss-slathered trees begin whispering your name and soft-bellied creatures follow the roll of your footsteps. Walk, and eventually you will come across a small clearing, its bushed life traded for a soupy mass of white, stardust flowers.

They were here once. All three of them. It was the day she left, the one of green skin and black eyes.

And if you brush your fingers across the petaled blanket, you will find a shell, jaded and too light for brush to properly hide it.

You will see the gaping hole where a neck once lived and the cracked peak that once carried a stubborn-souled girl.

It lies there, cradled in flower arms.

They left long ago.

CONTENTS

———

To those I glimpsed on street corners and sidewalks
who inspired whole characters, settings, or even
a breath of description—thank you.
And, of course, to the family who said, "Write your stories,"
and the friends who gave a template for such love.

AUTHOR'S NOTE

———

Wow! Hello! This is kind of crazy, that you're reading this. Reading my first novel!

Quite exciting.

I'd first like to thank you. I wrote the original short story, "Searching for the Sun," in my sophomore year of high school. We were reading Of Mice and Men in class, and let me tell you: I did not like it. I've read a few novels by John Steinbeck, and he is, well, a very descriptive author.

Though I did not particularly like the writing of his book, it is perhaps one of the most impressionable pieces of literature I have ever read. Specifically, Steinbeck focuses upon the friendship of Lennie and George, two complete opposites who share a desire to achieve the "American Dream" in the height of the Great Depression. This was the first time I'd ever read a book in which friendship was the main theme. There was no romance or dramatic violence (except accidents), no overthrowing of a massive superpower or coming of age tale, just two people against the woes of the land.

And within three days, twenty-one pages of my notebook were filled with the journey of Happy and Book. It wasn't until later I realized the correlation between my short story and Steinbeck's novel, but without that book, I doubt mine would ever have existed.

The original "Searching for the Sun" was the first piece of writing I felt was completely and wholly mine. Though I will heartily credit Steinbeck's lovely use of relationships as the inspiration for my indulgence in friendship, that is both the beginning and (thankfully) the end of our literary similarities. I wanted to take this unconditional, platonic love and throw it into a boiling pot of gothic fantasy. In crediting my love of this particular genre, I certainly cannot point to my reading prowess as a child, seeing as I loathed fantasy altogether and—I will shamefully admit—took pride in such a boycott.

Eventually I came to my senses, reading novels such as The Hobbit and Frankenstein (a book I am embarrassingly obsessed with). I learned about different platforms of storytelling such as animation, theater, and television. Simply, I consumed content, and all it took was Of Mice and Men to turn my head toward a story I can hardly believe I had the privilege of writing.

Throughout this book, you will notice a few things. Namely, the constant presence of death and its relationship with each individual character. Happy themself essentially is death, Book is dead, and Time is nearing death. Even the entire forest in which the novel is set shows a constant fear of death. This struggle with mortality—this inevitable ending—I placed into the hearts of each of my characters to express a question I've always worried over: what happens when we die?

I found the simple truth that death has the ability to twist its way through millions upon millions of different avenues of possibility. How can something exist and simply . . . not anymore? How does that make any sense? And in my novel, I answer that little question.

It doesn't!

It doesn't make sense. Death itself is infinite and boundaryless. We as living things can't possibly know the "after," as life shields us from that knowledge. I'd always struggled with this idea of the "next life" being so easy. So set and predetermined. We manage to tie death to life when they are so wholly separate from one another. There is no comfort in labeling death or searching for the place it will take us. It alienates us from life and makes us fret so much that we forget we're still breathing.

And what I want is to bridge that gap a little bit—to give death a voice that isn't sinister or domineering but innocent and gentle. Create this olive branch of communication between life and its end. Specifically, I use the mutual emotions of love and fear for both those alive and those dead.

Really, I do not know where this idea came from: where in my brain Happy existed, where I met Book and tasted the bitterness of her tragedy, what infallible dream or nightmare spurred the emotionless pining of The Man, or what everyday passerby molded Time. I'm still confused as to what gears in my imagination began turning themselves backward.

Perhaps its origins are as simple as the town I grew up in. A small, contentedly repetitive town. Despite this constant regularity, I've moved thirteen times in my eighteen years of life (I should mention that my parents are divorced, thus spurring such nomadic lifestyles). I once swore I'd lived in half our suburbia's neighborhoods and thus never had a desire to settle down. Though my novel is not the same as hopping a plane and flying wherever my savings take me, it is this idea that inspired the lack of a "base" in the novel.

Happy and Book do not need a home or a place to live, as they find that comfort in one another.

In the end, this book is about them. These two characters walking through a world they don't belong in, finding a sigh of solace in the company of one who is just as much an outcast as they are. It is hard to talk about the characters of my book without convincing myself they are real. I am simply the vessel in which these beings chose to speak their story.

So, really, it is my privilege to introduce you to Happy, Book, and whatever else you may find and hold on to.

Thank you for reading.

1

THE BEGINNING

———

A dead girl lay in the forest.

Her little body was nestled deep within a leafy maze of shadow and oak, past towering pines and gurgling brooks. Around a dead-end ravine, mountainous hill, and careening valley. Animal eyes flitted, blinking, frantically searching until the trees finally threw themselves open. Close, now.

At the revealed clearing's center dripped an inky pond, its pebbled shore straining toward a nervous willow tree whose leaves cracked in the chilled air. Forest creatures leaned forward, inhaling the near-imperceptible stench dribbling from its weight-leaden branches.

Yes, there she was, cast in shadow by the groggy blue sky.

Her limp, swinging frame trailed from a curving branch. A sweet girl. Buried in the crook of her neck and hidden beneath the fluffed coils of dark hair was a noose. Too bad, as it swelled the deep brown of her skin, creaking with the light strain of her body. A pretty girl, had it not been for that noose.

Beneath her lay a delicately veined scarlet flower, the sunset ring of its petals brazenly vibrant against the otherwise frosted ground.

As if agitated by some invisible hurricane, the dark pond waters tripped into a ripple, rolling up the trembling stone shore.

A tittering finch faltered and choked on its song, frail lungs heaving as watery ruffles lifted to waves. In an immediate decision of instinct, the bird turned, fluttering away as the forest flickered its leafy gaze toward the girl. The red flower shriveled into dust.

Disgusted by its compliant disruption of tangled legs, the breeze snatched itself from the girl as trees ceased their gossip and frogs skittered into the brush. There she hung, her puffed, cherry-red jacket trying desperately to veil the clogged bruises along her neck.

Silence reigned as the forest waited.

A collective, trembling breath disturbed the undergrowth as there rose from the pond a silhouette, trickling droplets steaming from Its rising form.

Its skin was black as the deepest, darkest ocean, where dreams lay buried and creatures swim with flesh of transparent nightmares. Standing perhaps eight feet tall, slits pulsed along Its webbed forearms. A fin-like horn curved from the top of Its head as wide, unblinking eyes glowed golden.

Turning in a slow circle, It stared into the cringing forest. Clouds swarmed over the sun as the being searched, raising an arm until a scythe-like appendage stitched above Its wrist unsheathed itself from the pond, tendrilled fingers slithering beneath it.

Upon seeing the girl, the being stalled and tilted Its lantern eyes, feeling a strange, wispy kind of wonder. The pond's ripples stagnated into a plate of solid glass as It strode carefully to shore, halting an arm's reach from her.

As the watery sun arched above, a tight clump of confusion knotted within the being's chest, as the girl did not look up or climb the tree or fly away. She did not fall beneath the lure of distant chirps or croaks, but remained a spinning ornament of gagged flesh, unperturbed by pointed scythes and glowing eyes.

And without such movement, It became a little nervous, uncommonly bemused. The being rubbed Its hands together as a whisper, raw and angry, poked at Its curious mind. It had been warned of such dangerous feelings and the consequences that followed them. Like a pounding drum of false obligation.

Warily, night descended.

After a quick glance toward Its blackening pond, the being dodged harsh whispers and reached for the girl, brushing the edged tip of their scythe against her cheek. A silent, wavering moment prevailed as It watched, the forest trees muffling their fearful cries.

A bursting scream ripped apart filmy sheens of wonder, nearly collapsing the being as invisible claws raked across Its eyes. Flung back by the physical shove of such internal noise, It scrabbled at Its head, gaze torn from the creaking girl as autumn leaves shrieked at Its careless footsteps. The outside world remained silent as It swung Its lanky frame and staggered beneath dark waters.

Not a splash echoed as the being slunk away, tormented by teeth-gleaming voices. And as the finned head descended, the forest sounds returned in a heaving sigh. What the being heard—those sweet, distant noises—were only a strum in a wonderfully immortal symphony.

There hung the girl, silent and still.

***

The next day, the pond and the trees and the animals continued their eternal, monotonous routines. The night had no stars, as the clouds had placed their stubborn hands across the sky, and instead the hours rolled by in tense silence, the breeze running off to a land without dead girls or decaying, sad smells.

As the shielded sunrise stretched its rayed arms, the being again rose from still waters, shoulders hunched. Dawn gagged as It walked across the glass-like water to stand before the unmoving girl.

Its glowing stare transfixed to the ancient willow behind her. Flaking wood shivered with a lasting breath, and the being raised Its scythe, touching the molding, sodden trunk. Branches folded in a vacuumed crack of sound and the poor, ragged tree collapsed.

A stillness draped across the forest with no origin and no ending. The kind that is always there, slung behind a sentence or woven deep within the fabric of skin. A forever kind of feeling.

It then crouched down, slicing through what little bit of dampened rope tethered the girl to the eroding willow, pulsing eyes unflinching. Incessant whispers flitted like white shadows across Its mind.

She refused to move. Yes, refused, as her rope was cut, freeing her little body from whatever might keep her still. The being hesitated, staring and wondering and thinking about things It had no right to. A hum of curiosity. Finally, seeing no ruffle from her jacket or quirk of her mouth, It made a choice. A decision quiet in its fervent trill of uncertainty. A pale flash of hissing voices.

It gazed at the loose ends of the girl's jeans, teetering at the line of finality before closing Its orbed, pulsing eyes. When It opened them, the girl blinked back, her pupils milky, puffy cotton clouds.

It jerked back, surprised. This was unexpected. Those crawling, inside voices had said she would sink like the willow, run away with bloated toes, or perhaps simply fall asleep like the other forest creatures did. She would be gone, one way or the other. But the girl had returned. She did not breathe, but her swollen, bulging eyes saw again.

The being stood rather abruptly; stared at the girl with twinkling, living eyes; and strode back into the pond.

It did not return for several more sunrises.

2

A NAME

What are you doing? There is nothing to leave for.

The being shook the edged voices away, rising from the pond on a crisp fall morning. Across stagnant water and leaning against the willow's bare retch of a stump sat the girl, leaves swirling around her like drunken fairies. After a brief, heavy moment of contemplation, It approached her, the sky a curved dome of clouds.

The noose hung around her neck like poorly handled jewelry, hair twisted into a spring of coils and fluffed above her head. Her blinking eyes appeared separate from an otherwise motionless body as the being neared and sat a polite distance away. Courteous, now that she made choices.

Its unblinking gaze shivered at the constant flash of skin that pressed against the girl's bleeding pupils, her eyelids nearly sticking to swollen cheeks.

You are sad. So easily shaken.

Looking away, It willed the weighted voice to cease as forest creatures rustled beneath green shadows, wary of such a golden-soaked stare. Grasses cracked in a flurry of terrified footsteps, and the being spun back, sensing Its blame. Yet as It again met the girl's flashing eyes, It found a winking light within her gaze, and unspoken words from a new voice bled into thought.

"Do you not like my blinking?" she asked, gaze scrunching.

Do not answer.

"Not particularly," replied the being, "but your hair is similar to dark chocolate."

"What is that?"

"I do not know, but there is a Man who once adored it."

The girl cocked her head slightly. "That's nice."

"I suppose it is."

A light, trickling sensation curved down Its back, mind now silent of this pressing new voice. A contented kind of silence, where words are expected to follow. It was a secret, unspoken sound, and both were eager to continue this talking-but-not-talking as the girl's eyes settled upon a more rhythmic pace. The being leaned forward, intrigued by the established formality of kindness.

"What do you think I look like?" It asked, folding webbed hands beneath Its chin.

It seemed the girl had just discovered she could see. "Well, you have no hair—" she said.

"That is true."

"—or ears."

It nodded.

"You look like the forest doesn't want you," she finished.

"Is that a bad thing?" the being asked, glancing at their scythe.

"No, because the forest doesn't want me either."

"At least we have that in common."

"Yes, that's more important than chocolate hair, I think."

With a light twitch, the girl smiled. The being tensed Its sloped shoulders, startled to watch her do such a thing so soon after friendship's inflation. Never had It seen teeth so flat and thus did not understand an edgeless smile's meaning. Memories splashed into Its thoughts. Branches cut clean by such a smile.

It scrambled back, stopped only by the concerned furrow of the girl's brows. Shaking those lantern eyes in a desperate ache for trust, It pushed against a desire for panicked escape, tapping Its fingers.

"Why did you do that just now?" It whispered.

Her fluffed hair fell forward. "What did I just do?"

"Your mouth tilted and your teeth showed."

"Oh," she said, pushing the hair from her eyes, "I don't know exactly why, but I was happy, so I think it may be because of that."

The being, almost sheepish, crawled back. "That is good. I was worried."

The rope easily engulfed the girl's neck. "Why?"

"I thought you might have begun to not like me or that perhaps you would recoil like the forest things do."

"I would never do that. I'm not one of the forest things," she said, eyes squinting. "I'm talking to you, aren't I?"

Perhaps It would bring a flat-toothed smile. "You are right. You are wiser than your appearance lets on, girl."

A sudden, sprinkled frown. "Do I not have a name?" she asked.

"When I first saw you, you never mentioned one."

"Well, I don't fancy being called 'girl'," she said, lifting her chin. "We can make you a name, too, if you'd like?"

And so they started their first adventure, and It felt another emotion so new that if Its skin were anything but ocean black, It would have paled.

Sadistic thing! Selfish, wretched thing, to create your own autonomy.

After much deliberation, the two decided the webbed, long-legged being would be called Happy, as that is what the girl most felt around them. Her name took more thinking, until at last they decided upon Book; for Happy, again remembering The Man and his lessons full of sharpened teeth, recalled his affinity for how a Book told stories and gave advice and was always in his head, even when he left for distant lands.

While discussing such pressing issues as names and memories, Happy moved closer to Book, knees wrapped within spider arms and the scythe carefully tucked behind their back. She was not afraid, and Happy felt that as her friend, they should never be far away.

But when the sun, held behind a mist of clouds, began to set, Happy forced themself back into the pond. No emotion, no matter how strong, can convince the skies to turn directions. And though Time to them was meaningless and the skies would inevitably lighten, Happy whispered in their head, "Good night," and eagerly awaited morning.

You disgusting, filthy Creature.

3

HUMAN MAN

He slouched upon the ground, blistered by the singeing heat of his own confidence. Through shadowed breaks in the trees, he watched the Creature talk to her. To that girl. The Man trembled at his foolishness. Oh, what to do now.

***

Hush now. You do not know him. Do not assume the words he would like spoken.

His hands are bone. Skin stuffed with the wool of marrow and blood. Go on. Rip him open and see what you find.

He hates his eyes, more so the veins beneath them. The delicately sewn glare cannot portray his shame in blinking. The loathing in squinting up toward a sky he once lived in.

Here is one thing to tell. A gooey, delicious secret.

He is hurting. Broken for so long, curing him is a waste. What does a beaten dog fight with but tooth and claw?

But if the mutt could stand and take the whip, would it see then? See the frantic reverie of slashing burns? A pain for once not its own? A shared bond of hatred.

Is this better than freedom? There is joy—surely joy is there, or else such lashes would not be given—and what of freedom if its fruits have already rotted?

But he is not a dog.

The Man is mortally, utterly, dejectedly lost. Screaming at a pain he refuses to understand, snapping his whip at golden eyes of warmth and emotion. He is a snarling animal, feverish and hateful. Yet that poor lantern gaze The Man can't bear to meet sees an anger so craftily prescribed, they believe it wrapped in the cardinal bow of compassion. The whip hits again and again.

What if I told you it was forever ago when this began? That his arm has yet to tire?

Wait. Stop for a moment. I feel your judgment oozing along the carved rivers of his cheeks. I feel it bubble and churn across the mucus-lined pit of his stomach.

Stay quiet. Listen closely, and perhaps you will learn something. Look again at the sunken wretch of his face. Look at those scars. Those gushing waters.

Oh, the glory of tears and pain. So permanent.

He has done many things. He is a monster, screaming himself raw with mortal lungs and fragile tendons.

He brings the whip down, and sobs.

4

ADVENTURE MAKING

———

The browned forest sighed in resignation upon Happy's arrival the next morning. Birds had fled from their nests and trees hung snow-dusted blankets around their shoulders as the sun again refused to shine. Happy's webbed footsteps softened against a rug of leaves thickened by the still air's inability to blow it away.

Everything will crumble in your selfish hands.

The voice was fainter. Diminished and small.

"Hello," Happy said upon reaching Book.

She smiled, craning her head upward to meet their tilted gaze.

"Hello," she responded. "Why do you step into the pond every night?"

"I do not know," they replied, sitting down. "But something tells me I have to."

"Does it speak like I do?"

"No. Not really. It tugs."

Book's light-filled gaze sparked. "That doesn't sound nice."

Happy leaned back, surprised. "It is all I have ever known," they explained quietly, a distant rustle of some fleeing animal tripping their words.

"So you must listen to it because it's all that's there?"

"I guess," they said slowly, "but I am no longer sure."

"Yes, for I am here now. I must complicate things," Book said, reaching for the tangled rope cinched to her neck.

"Maybe, but never in a bad way."

Book again smiled, looking out at the slumping trees gathered beyond the pond's shore. Their leafless trunks gathered in a clumped, paranoid way, as if the mottled flecks of light bouncing throughout the forest might sharpen and slice off their branches.

She turned back toward her lightless friend. "What is behind those trees?" she asked.

Happy thought for a moment. "The sun. Behind the trees is the sun."

"Is it far?"

"Perhaps."

Book jostled the rope with an excited shrug of her shoulders. "We should go and find it."

Happy glanced back at the pond for only a moment. "I agree," they said. "Let us be the first to find the sun."

"How might we be the first?" Book asked, sniffing with curiosity.

"I have a feeling we will be the first to try."

"Is it that same feeling telling you to go into the pond every night?" she asked, suddenly wary.

"No," Happy assured her. "No, this is a different feeling."

She pulled at her muddy jeans. "Good, because I don't think I much like the feeling telling you to leave. It seems like a bad feeling."

She lasted a fraction of my eternity!

Happy scratched at the back of their head. "How so?" they asked.

Book shifted, her cherry-red jacket lightly dusted in frost and mud. "Well, it doesn't seem that you like going into the pond every night. It seems you are told to go, and so you must."

"I am perhaps told," Happy responded, their words an automatic rush, "and perhaps I have no choice, but the feelings are quite ancient, you see, and they know much more than I. I listen because someone chooses to help me. To tell me of the things I do not know."

"But when we go looking for the sun, and we've traveled far from the pond, where will you go then?"

Happy searched Book's bleeding, dark eyes. "I do not know. The feelings may tell me."

"And if not?"

"In that case, I will stay with you, if you do not mind."

"Of course not, Happy!" cried Book, opening her little hands. "You are my friend, and I don't think I could ever turn you away."

I will tell you the truth you blind yourself from.

Finding the sun was an ambitious journey, and one of many sacrifices. The two, beneath the shadow of a cloudy sky, decided that Happy must—unfortunately—retreat to the pond until yellow rays dared wander again, allowing Book to determine where the sun went to rest.

"It can't be much different from a pond," she'd told Happy, eyes wide. "Any sleeping thing can hide underwater, for the land never bothers to look beneath it. I know this because sometimes, when you are late to arrive, a fluffy-tailed creature will spring across that little group of trees there." And she pointed toward a place Happy had not before noticed, for they never ventured to a place that was in no need of their venturing.

After Book saw the sun's fiery travels, Happy could return, and off they'd go. But Happy did not want to leave for so long. To sit in silent waters, counting the bubbles following a twitch of their scythe-like extension. To listen to the voices scream for them to stay. To wait for Book, their friend, who was forced to watch the sky alone.

Happy knew of their friend's fears. Of the trees and the fluffy-tailed creatures. It seemed the forest had yet even to look at her, as if holding a ragged intake of breath.

Standing in the growing dusk, Happy caught a distant flicker in Book's gaze.

"I will come back," they whispered to her. Sometimes there is no goodness in leaving. No assurance a golden-eyed being can offer.

"Of course," she answered, clutching the rope.

"And you will not leave until my return."

"Of course."

Happy nodded. "And then we will find the sun."

"Yes," she managed.

"Good night, Book. I will see you soon."

"Good night, Happy. I love you."

Happy about-faced, holding their stomach as they dipped beneath the ripple-less pond, straining to recall what The Man had said about "love." Memory's dredges held nothing but a dark maze, oozing the word "lost" from its slick walls.

***

Happy wondered what it was like to sleep as floating green particles foamed around them, their webbed feet brushing the carpeted pond floor. They spun in a slow, methodical circle, thick water breezing past as Happy's orbed, pulsing eyes turned to a sky they could not see, waiting for the water to lighten.

A constant scream skipped between rising bubbles, enhanced by the underwater silence. Flaring and beating at Happy's averted gaze.

Don't leave! You don't know what you're doing. You can't do this. Failure!

Perhaps Happy wasn't sure where their next footsteps might lead them, but that was no longer a bad thing. Because there was Book. They had a friend where before were only trees and endings.

Happy stretched forth a hand just before the water's break as the voices cracked against their autonomous desires. Raising their scythe before them, Happy pushed against the static wall of disappointment, and a grainy shame slowly filled their gills. In the fuzzed, nearly indiscernible words, Happy caught a memory's flash of sharp teeth. Haunted movements and scarred cheeks. Automatically, they drew their hand away and succumbed to a temporary boil of blame and disdain.

Oh, what would The Man say if he knew?

***

Book practiced moving her stiff and purple limbs, blinking in shock when they did what she told them to. The trees whispered about her at night, curdling the darkness as if their mockery would convince the poor girl to run away.

What had she done in her short waking existence to offend them so harshly? Poking in her mind, Book searched for memories that didn't exist, as if banging desperately against a metal box she knew to be empty. She shrank into her jacket, too overwhelmed by living noises to question the origins of such fabric.

The cacophony of returned forest creatures stacked into a lilting tower, jabbing the sky with their needle-sharp voices and rapping against Book's ears until their gushing cries pounded within her chest. Until she begged to scream with the collapsed tendons of her vocal cords.

Daring a glance at the sky, Book flinched as though the stretchy gray clouds had burst and collapsed atop her. She wheezed for useless breath, clutching the rope. Her bulging eyes swerved frantically, landing upon a ripple emanating from the pond's center. Book loosened the clench of her fingers, reminded of Happy's kind words. Of their adventure and the sun she was tasked with finding.

She turned back to the suddenly unpunctured sky, enduring whatever taunts the forest things could think of, waiting for daylight.

5

FINDING THE SUN

———

The sun took its brush of fire and dipped it into an earth-tinged paint of shadows, leading a pale-yellow line through crisp winter skies.

The forest barely took notice of the crowding morning light. No flowers splayed greedy petals. No birds whistled through their triangle beaks. No fluffy-tailed creatures sniffled awake.

Only Book reacted to the strong, distant beams, swollen eyes squinted and hands grasping at her puffed jacket zipper.

Waiting for dusk, she tracked its golden stroke, lips trembling. Perhaps the sun would catch a glimpse of her bubbled neck and run away, disgusted even way high up upon its throne. So Book did not stretch, but watched and waited, eyes burning.

At twilight's gleam, the sun crawled into a pond far beyond the trees. A pond that Book could not see but was positive existed. As darkness blanketed the shriveled forest, she called out to her friend.

"Happy! Happy, the sun has come! I know now where to go!"

Happy burst from the glass-like water and strode toward her, the forest things offering only a dejected sigh at their return. Their skin blurred in the steam of sizzling droplets as Happy sat before Book.

"What does *love* mean?" they asked, their frame solidifying and startling Book out of her excitement. Stars spied from their light-year vanities.

"Why do you want to know?"

Happy widened their eyes, molding the darkness around them. "Because that is what you said to me before we had to wait for the sun."

"Well, that was a long Time ago."

Happy nodded in understanding. "So it no longer matters."

"No!" Book nearly shouted, holding up her hands. "Of course it does. It's just hard to explain."

"Why?"

"Because I don't know what it is, but I know what it feels like."

Happy shivered. *Love* sounded rather knotted in its beauty. "Can you explain the feeling?" they asked.

"I can try." Book glanced up at the glittery stars, thinking. "When you come out of the pond, I feel it. I think it's because I know you are coming to be with me." She regarded their lantern stare. "It's almost overwhelming, the feeling. It beats slow and constant, but sometimes when you say something nice, it speeds up and I feel a pouring, soft warmth"—she tapped her hand across her chest—"like this. And sometimes . . . sometimes it's scary, and I'd prefer it to go away. When you go into the pond, the feeling still pours, but it pours like ice."

Happy leaned forward and touched the coiled springs of Book's hair, as close as they could get to physical comfort. Fleeting, as if she might revert to living flesh beneath their fingers. Faintly, Book recalled the collapsed willow, vulnerable to a brush of Happy's scythe. But this was merely hair, and it would stay that way, devoid of consequence for her friend who seemed so fearful of mistakes.

"Well, then I think I feel it also," Happy said, drawing their fingers back.

"Truly?"

"Truly. And I am glad that I do, because if you felt it all alone, I am sure you would soon become sad, and I know sadness is a rather bad feeling."

Book smiled, tears glittering upon the edges of her bloated eyes. And before Happy could react, apologize for whatever wrong they believed they committed, the forest, in one moment, leaned in close to the girl, deeply inhaling those watery eyes.

Trees do not see tears as dead things.

For such willful, unconscious treason to instinct's carved stone pillars, the forest soon snapped away in a torrent of ground-shaking disgust. Trees rounded on one another, screeching against the damnation of such yearning. Terrified, wretched cries ripped at the two cowering friends.

Keep away! screeched the forest. *Away! Away!*

Then it stopped, the mossy ground grew still, and dawn sent night hissing beyond the horizon.

Happy and Book stared out in wide-eyed shock, shaking as the tremors fizzled away. The creeping hatred of the forest things burned both their hands.

Book's trifling tears fell in the quiet.

***

Happy cradled their scythe against their chest, terrified they might brush against the now stagnant branches. Their memories dribbled with mistakes, at disappointment and the consequences to come of them.

They stood as Book wiped at her cheeks, desperate to relieve the cavernous worry opening beneath her milky pupils.

"Which direction did the sun go, Book?" Happy asked.

She pointed, elbow cracking.

"I think we should go now," they said, "while the forest is sleeping." Happy was hesitantly persistent, willing Book's gaze to lift. "Let us go now. Let us go on our adventure."

"What if we come across another forest?" she asked timidly.

"I have no doubt we will, but we are going together. The trees will not dare come close to us."

Finally, she met Happy's worried eyes. "Alright," she said.

Throughout the countless seasons of their existence, Happy had never learned what, exactly, their purpose was. Had never known the results of their actions or the reasons for doing them. They were told only of directions and their failure in execution.

But now they had friendship and reciprocated love and the leaking excitement of choice. Happy didn't understand the end they brought to the forest creatures, as there no longer seemed a reason for it. Book turned, resting against her straightened arms.

For once, Happy did not feel selfish in their reach for a purpose, but eager and light. As if waking from dreams they imagined having. Briefly, they wondered of The Man's reaction, what his spiked teeth might say.

But The Man knew of everything and would surely understand.

After a moment, Book managed to stand upon the muddy stilts of her legs, hands flung to the sides. She nodded to Happy and glanced at the gills along their arms, the distraction briefly tinging future troubles with a clumsy stroke of whimsy.

"Those slits in your arms?" she asked, lifting her feet warily.

"Yes?" said Happy, looking down at their lanky forearms.

"What are they for?"

"I do not know, but they make me feel better in the pon—in the water."

Book swung a leg forward as the morning sky again clouded. "Will you use them on our adventure?"

"No, I will not."

The voice landed a vengeful finger upon the edges of Happy's consciousness.

Wait for—

They pushed away the accusatory hand, and words dropped away.

***

And off they went to find the sun. They had no possessions, and so carried no burden. Their pace was purposeful in its slowness, allowing the tepid forest things to run away.

They sat upon the ground of new places once night fell, playing at the game of rest. Book told of emotions with no origin and Happy ran a long, curious finger across fallen leaves, casting their lantern eyes out into the darkness. This went on for several more weeks.

6

STARTING THE JOURNEY

———

The forest was continuously morphing, weaving itself by the threads of new roots and dirt at each gentle step upon winter's palm. After a stilted day hobbling through a growing barrage of rocks, Happy and Book traveled into the weary fronds of dusk. Birds did not chirp above them, and the wind still ran far ahead, keeping its breezy legs away from such swollen skin and golden eyes.

Silence reigned but for footsteps and a humming rush beating throughout the forest. Happy watched Book totter between stones, her hold tight around the rope upon her neck. Her purple, snakelike bruises played within the dips beneath her eyes.

The rushing noise steadily grew. Perhaps The Man had come. This was his way of warning. Of saying hello.

Trilling with guilty paranoia, Happy climbed a bare-chested rock, peering into the gathering darkness. Mountainous trees leaned between boulders and crunchy grass patches, green nettles encompassing their circling branches. Ahead, the foliage thinned frighteningly quickly, the ground nearly swallowed by rock.

"Book," said Happy, stretching their webbed feet back upon the uneven ground.

"Yes, Happy?" she replied, stopping the lolling swing of her legs.

"Do you hear a noise?"

"I do."

Happy nodded.

"It is as if fire could roar," they said.

Book dared a couple of steps, her coiled hair masking the furrow of her brow.

"What's *fire*?" she asked.

"I am not sure," Happy pondered, "but I think it burns. It has light, but not like the sun's."

"Do you think the noise is fire?" Book asked, mouth dropping to a frown.

"No," said Happy, "but I worry he has come to get me."

Book glanced back at them. "Is it The Man? The one who loved a different Book?"

"Yes," Happy replied, hesitating. "He is like fire."

"How so?"

Happy stilled the tremble of their hands, shocked by their own awe.

"He can do whatever he wishes, as there is no will he bends to. The Man knows of everything and refuses to run from it."

Book hesitated, releasing the rope. "Why would he come for you?" she whispered, her voice grating.

"He is all I have ever known."

Book stared, incredulous. "That's not an answer."

"I know no other one."

"Happy," said Book, continuing forward.

"Yes, Book?" Happy responded, following behind her.

"How long have you known him?"

"He created me."

They continued in silence, nearing the roaring, fiery sound. Mist soaked deep beneath the now sparse trees around them, fogging the land ahead.

The noise rushed and pounded against slack boulders. Happy, shamed by anticipation, examined the watery dust that floated upon Book's hair, searching for an apology. They opened their thoughts, but Book gasped as the land dropped into a gaping cliff, algae carpeting the otherwise sharp ledge. She staggered back, nearly toppling into the ravine.

"Book! Are you alright?" cried Happy, reaching out impulsively before snatching the scythe back, glinting in the pale light.

Upon regaining her balance, Book looked at them and smiled, pointing down below.

"I think this is where sound lives," she said.

Happy stepped beside her, gaping at the ground far, far below. Tendrilled bushes poked beneath a cloudlike fog while thin, intricately tied trees scattered across the layered rock walls. A gushing fall of water spewed at the rounded end of the cliff opposite them.

"Happy?" said Book, staring at the beating, eternally powerful falls.

"Yes, Book?"

She pointed toward the elegantly powerful stream.

"He's not here."

Sour memories, spoiled by adventures and friendship, dribbled between Happy's fingers.

"No, he is not," they whispered.

The two stood as night swung its starry dress over the ravine. Book rocked upon stiffening legs as Happy leaned forward into the spiraling mist.

Beauty was found in the cool presses of the falls, the constant bend and flow, the crashing roar that seemed more eternal than sunlight or fires. Flashy breaths of past things played in the darkness.

"I feel wrong," Happy whispered, taking a jagged step back.

Book looked up at them, the remnants of wonder lightening her gaze. "What do you mean?" she asked.

Happy tore their eyes from the crashing symphony below. "Something inside of me will not go away. Like I am two instead of one."

"Does it feel like pain?"

"No." Happy's scythe curved toward the ground. "It is as if I am wishing for that which I do not want. It pounds every Time I make a decision."

Book's eyes fell to her hands, clasped together. "Do you no longer want to find the sun with me, Happy?" she breathed.

"Quite the opposite. It is the only thing I want," said Happy, "but my head tells me horrible things. Says I am bad for leaving."

"Happy," said Book, her voice filled with innocent wisdom, "I think that might be The Man."

"Why would he hurt me?" they said, voice sparked by desperation. "Why does he fill me with emotions I would rather not feel?"

"I don't know, Happy. I'm sorry."

"It is alright," they assured her, for Book never carried with her pointed teeth and scarred eyes.

After another moment, the two turned away from the cliff and the worlds below them.

"Do you know of people like him?" asked Happy, beginning the long trek around the ravine.

Book quirked her head. "From before I met you?"

"Yes."

"That's it," she said, following beside Happy, "I don't think there was anything before I opened my eyes and saw you and the pond."

"Nothing?"

"I'm not sure, as I began only when I could see. I haven't even a glimpse of what might have been."

"I am sorry," said Happy, as they believed that was what needed saying.

"What for?"

"I guess because there is something you are not sure existed."

Book smiled. "Well, Happy, it seems I'm better off not knowing. I would not like there to be two of me."

Happy nodded. The falls settled its noise beside them.

They continued deep into the night, until grass dried and rocks sank beneath thick-rooted trees. As ghostly stars hung beyond wispy clouds, Happy and Book lay within a narrow clearing, silent and calm.

The roaring water sang around them like a tangy, ever-present memory.

7

RED FLOWER

The flower appeared quietly next to Happy's scythe. They watched its delicately veined petals grow and spread into a velvet fountain of red, stretching from a black-ember center. Another sprouted not ten feet away, just a breath deeper into the forest.

It cannot be right, for flowers to grow so near their ends.

Happy gaped, narrowing their golden eyes as a flaming path streaked its way through thick, needled branches. A mesmerizing lull flowed through them, pressing against Happy's hidden sores of guilt. Constricted their malleable resolve. They turned to Book, finding her fingers twiddling the rope.

"Book."

Her hands stalled. "Yes, Happy?"

"I think I must go do something."

"Where are you going?" she asked as Happy stood.

"I do not know"—they pointed at the flower next to them, Book's gaze following—"but a living thing is next to my hand." They did not bother mentioning The Man. How his pale hands knew of many talents. It would only upset her.

She glared at the red petals, a strange, crinkled expression souring her stare. She sat up, frost crackling on her jacket.

"I don't understand why you must follow them. What have the living things done for you?" she said.

"Nothing yet. They have never tried to touch me before." Happy turned to the sprouting trail of flowers, entranced.

"How long will you be gone?"

"I do not know."

"Happy, what if they take you away?" said Book, her voice rising.

"I do not think they want to keep me." No longer did it feel as though they talked of flowers.

"It will not be like when we waited for the sun to relight the sky, will it? It won't be that long?"

Happy looked to her, briefly shaken from their excitement. "When we waited for the sun, the living things scorned us," they said. "Now, they call to me. It is too different for it to be the same."

"But you're leaving."

"For only a little while."

Happy refused to think of their words as a lie. Their sick hope to find him did not birth truth. Did not create words worth speaking. And though weakened by the pull of fiery petals, Happy leaned upon the strength of friendship, as value was now measurable beyond the instinctual touch of their scythe. Fear was no longer a solitary experience.

"Book," said Happy, "a few flowers will not cause me to forget our journey."

"I trust you. Just . . ." She finally met those golden eyes. "Please don't leave me for too long."

"Of course."

Happy turned to the icy forest, stepping carefully beyond flaming red flowers. Their shoulders skimmed the bellies of tree branches and leaves sucked themselves deep within the dark canopy above. Silence festered as nearby fluffy-tailed creatures tripped over their stumpy legs and hopped away, either from black webbed feet or the direction those feet were headed.

***

Trees leaned upon his shoulders, brushing their mighty limbs against his ankles as The Man clicked his tongue, waiting.

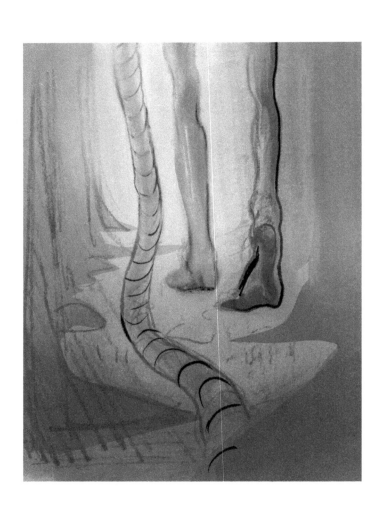

8

ROPE

A Long-Ago Day:

He did it on a glaringly sunny morning. The clear sky was a whitewashed mirror as he walked through a field of tall grass, forcing dry stems to grasp at his ankles and rip themselves from the ground.

He didn't think much of it, only that it was such an empty pleasure to feel the pull on his feet tug and give way.

Do not ask why. The Man does not like when he is asked questions.

The Creature was new and festering in that pond, its gangly body towering over him, those eerily large eyes above his forehead. It asked too many questions. Too many to allow for any sort of caution-less freedom. The Man felt the frailest twinge of guilt whenever thinking of the pond. How he kept the Creature there, sunken beneath a murky cave.

He stopped, grass slithering up his legs as he grew them beyond intention. A billowing wind rippled across the field like a collective, dried wave.

The solid forest wall rose a short distance from him, spilling its cool green shadows. Glaring at it for a hateful moment, The Man then turned around, clenching veined hands.

He needed this. Had to keep this up or they would never bother with him. The Creature was small. Its feelings nonexistent.

Running back the way he'd come, The Man tripped over himself in grabbing at torn strands of grass until all he could smell were their sweetened blades.

He dropped to the ground, fumbling with the panicked scribbles of an idea as the sun beat above him, rugged dirt jabbing at his knees. Within his pale hands writhed a thin, lengthy bundle, held so tightly the stems nearly withered away.

The grass clustered together as he grasped at either side and twisted.

Sweat clawed across his wan face.

He toiled with the folded bundle, bending its compressing form until it thinned into a rope, faltering as he ran out of churned grass before stabbing at the blades next to him.

It was done. Faster than The Man anticipated. His teeth, sharpened into blades, cut into his reddened lips. Taking a moment to calm himself, he brushed the grime from his hair and flicked off stray pieces of earth stuck to his legs, wiping the saliva and blood from his mouth.

He stood, training his stride toward the pond, which was hidden deep beneath the leafy canopy of trees ahead.

The rope dragged behind him.

9

LYING TEETH

———

As the soft crunch of their footsteps faded into a dull beat of consistency, Happy reached the last flower. A voice wove through the unfamiliar darkness.

"You were not at the pond."

Their eyes shot up, captured by The Man's contemptuous gaze. The nettled trees bent heavily inward, caressing his ghostly pale skin. Happy slouched beneath The Man's glare. Trickling scars lined both his cheeks, and trailing vines marked the bend of his knees.

"Yes," Happy whispered.

"Did you simply leave?"

What were they to say? Words were an independence now, sloshing into a foamy river of opinion. Happy used them to speak things that mattered. No longer could they remember how to satisfy The Man's bitter thoughts.

"No, it is not simple," Happy replied finally.

The Man flashed the jagged points of his teeth. "Are you telling me you abandoned everything for the mere explanation of complexity?" he snarled.

"No." Doubt crawled beneath Happy's intentions, infesting their desire to explain with the need for self-preservation. Perhaps it would be a good thing, to show him what had happened. Happy was gifted with purpose, and The Man's extraordinary knowledge of everything would surely permit him to understand.

But The Man had begun pacing, running veined hands through his hair.

Fog curled around their feet, circling them like a transparent whirlpool.

"Why are you so selfish?" he nearly shouted, throwing back his head. "I didn't bring you into existence to play games that satisfy your emptiness. You have no will! No right, no desire, no—"

"I have a name."

For a moment, he was still. Fog rose toward their knees as The Man stalled, facing Happy.

"You have no right to a name."

"A girl gave it to me," Happy continued, straightening their cowering shoulders. "You should meet her. She is small, but a sound in her voice makes me feel better than when she is not there."

"You have no right to know anyone but me."

Happy wasn't listening to him and his bad intentions. "My name is Happy, because that is what the girl feels when she sees me."

Happy had never seen The Man with such shock in his eyes.

"She has a rope like you do," they finished, clasping their hands together.

The Man dropped his voice to a chilling whisper. "You do not understand what she is."

"She is Book, just like the one you showed me."

A thickened dread spilled into Happy's words as they forged on, desperate to avoid the monstrous possibilities in silence.

"She has blinking eyes," they continued, peering at The Man, "but they close more than yours do."

"How dare—"

"You said bad things would happen if I left."

His creased brow chiseled with anger. "They will."

"Why haven't they happened yet?" A mistake.

The Man opened his razor-lined mouth and Happy felt an emotion Book had not yet spoken of. A dense rumbling of ash and hot coal. Before those needle teeth made way for tongue and sound, Happy barreled forward. "You tell me to not ask questions, but I ask Book things and she answers. I thought you were the only one who could do that?"

"What makes you think her answers are true?" he whispered, spitting on the iced forest floor.

Happy waited a moment, allowing themself the wonder in speaking such a truth. "Because she is my friend," they whispered, "and it would be rude to think otherwise."

"You are a fool."

"You are a *liar.*"

Their confidence drained beneath them. *Liar.* A word Happy never thought they'd have the courage to say. A terrible word.

But was it worse to avoid true things, thus maintaining whatever illusion binds two hands and calls it freedom?

The Man staggered toward Happy, trees springing back into their natural positions, nettles falling to the ground in a clustered rush. Panic seized Happy's golden eyes. They needed Book. She would tell them what to do. Happy needed their friend.

Leave.

Yet as they backed away, a leathered root jumped from the ground and they plunged to the life-covered earth.

Too close! So much breath and air and existence. Happy snatched in their scythe, reeling at the screeching grasses. The final red flower glared just next to their shivering frame.

Human eyes again met Happy's, so much closer now as The Man crouched in front of them. He smiled, teeth shining with disappointment.

"Why do you say that? Why do you say such nasty things?" he soothed, grabbing Happy's cradled scythe. Pulled it toward him. "Has she corrupted you so quickly?" Slowly, he ran a finger across the sharpened appendage. Not touch, but an observation.

"I am different now," stuttered Happy.

"Yes, you poor Creature," The Man whispered, setting his palms on either side of Happy's head. His gaze turned curious, searching. "Why can I not hear you?"

"I do not understand."

"No matter. Obviously it was not working."

"Is there something—"

"I fear for you," The Man said. "You cannot begin to imagine what is to come of this."

"What will come?"

"Too many things to explain." He dropped his hands, frowning. In a cracking strain of joints, The Man stood and turned away. "If you return to the pond, perhaps it will go back. Change poisons our idea of the past. It distorts the necessity of the future."

"But I am different."

"Yes, and all you must do is go back. Go back and you will be fixed," The Man said, glancing over his shoulder at Happy, nearly invisible by fog and darkness. "You are so broken. It hurts to watch your suffering."

Happy sat up, grasping their legs and craning desperate golden eyes toward The Man. Their webbed feet curled beneath them, rattled by a leaked yearning. An aching hope for praise.

Lifting his swollen lips, The Man sneered, walking into the shadow-soaked brush. Happy waited until his footsteps faded before looking again to the red flower. Its petals dribbled like a bloodied cloth. The Man's touch lingered, his words echoing like the voices that once plagued Happy. Upon standing, they held their scythe aloft, trembling at their inability to rip it from their wrist.

Slowly, they turned and began walking back, driven by a need to apologize. To bring about a new memory devoid of loathing and shame.

***

Happy traversed dew-tinged grasses, the pond seething in their memory. In spotting a puffed, cherry-red jacket beyond a rasping bunch of thickets, they allowed themself to understand that it was The Man who'd kept them beneath such waters.

Happy made another choice: they would not go back.

10

DECAYING FRIEND

The falls' gentle rumble hummed throughout the forest as Happy returned. Book lay upon the moistened ground, face concealed within the wreath of her hair.

The scythe glared into Happy's giant eyes as they sat across from her. Memories flashed before them.

All you must do is go back.

Turning sharply from the poisoned words, they leaned forward. "I have returned," they whispered, searching for Book's gaze.

"Yes, I can see that," she said, rolling away.

Happy scrutinized their open palms, thrown by Book's clear dismissal. A cautious insect flicked at the strings of its hushed song. "What did you do while I was away?" they asked timidly, pressing their hands behind them to avoid the scythe's taunting.

Book shrugged. "I walked in a circle."

"That is nice."

"No, it was not." She glowered then, singeing Happy's lantern gaze. "I was alone and it was terrible, and the forest things mocked me when I fell down."

Happy jolted. "You fell?"

A spray of sticks and mud flaked from Book's chocolate hair as she sat up, glowering into her lap. Happy shivered, toes iced in guilt as the clouded sun rose and tossed light upon them.

"I am sorry I was not here to help you," they said finally, cracking the stifling silence.

"What could you have done, Happy?" Book sighed, a splash of dirt streaking across her swollen cheek.

Happy tucked their scythe further behind them, flinching at the phantom press of earth against their back and the slithering motion of a tree root.

"You are right," they said. "But it would have been better. Perhaps the forest would not have been so cruel."

"Yes," she replied bitterly. "While they fear you, they hold only hate for me."

Another wrenching squeeze within their chest. Happy did not respond, instead touching a splotch of mud upon the edge of Book's hair in a tender olive branch.

She sniffed away her tears.

"Those red flowers?" Happy whispered, wiping at the clumped earth. "The ones that look like a sunrise? They brought me to The Man, Book."

"Did they?" she said dully.

"Yes."

"And what did The Man say to you, Happy? Did he teach you of more things?" A hazy suspicion darkened the lilt in her voice.

Slowly, Happy drew their fingers away, flicking their golden eyes into the leaning trees around them. "He told me things, certainly."

"Well, that's good."

You do not understand what she is.

"Book?" said Happy, looking down.

The rope dangled off her shoulder. "Yes, Happy?"

"I will always come back."

"Come back from what?"

The heat of shame dragged its flaming tongue across Happy's midnight skin. "The flowers," they said, "and I am sorry I was gone so long."

Book squeezed the rope's end, eyes squinting. "I want to be angry," she whispered.

Acknowledging her disappointment with a slump of their lengthy spine, Happy nodded. "I know."

"But I don't think I can," she continued, her words soft. "It hurts too much, to think of you leaving."

"Then think of my return."

She smiled a strange, distorted sort of smile. "We both know I'm not so patient."

**

Morning light soon poked through the clouds, drawing the two friends back within the puffed trail of their journey.

They walked for many days in silence.

Waiting, perhaps, for sunrise flowers to bloom upon Happy's hands. They were not angry. The cloth of silence is never a furious thing unless a muffled blemish lies within its folds.

Yet concern bubbles and pops until boiling over, soiling the cloth and its masked stains entirely.

Because Book had fallen, and nothing Happy could do could stop that from happening again.

Nothing to set her upright.

11

WHITE FLOWERS

———

Freshly budded grass flattened beneath the padding caution of Happy's feet, a warmed humidity slouching the now pale tree branches above. Troves of white flowers bloomed in the sparse canopies, fanned by thick-handed leaves.

The towering, nettled trees had faded along with winter as Happy and Book tottered forward, each swollen step led by the draining hope that another would follow. Book's legs, purple and near bursting whenever she dared stand, swelled beneath the dirty fabric of her jeans.

Sad, to watch the end creep back toward victory.

Happy tried not to look at such crooked feet. Tried to think of nice things to make their friend smile away the apprehension. Things The Man had told them of in a drippy kind of voice. But Happy did not like reminders of The Man anymore. They had a dreadfully thick kind of guilt, tainting thought's foggy breath with images of ponds and abandoned obligations. Yet Happy allowed the memories to simmer and dull the smell of rot and decay.

"Book?" they asked, ducking beneath a low-hanging branch.

"Yes, Happy?"

"I am having trouble."

Lifting her gaze from the spongy forest floor, Book frowned. "What's troubling you?"

Happy did not understand secrets. The Man never kept them. "I want to think of good things so you will not wish for working legs," they said.

"Working legs are for living things."

"Yes," they persisted, waving away the contented resignation in her voice, "but there are things meant for us. Things we are allowed to want. I would rather you think of those."

Book's eyes had changed, too. Black, bleeding pupils now held within them the crease of understanding as she looked to Happy.

"I don't think there is anything I want."

Happy clasped their hands together, wrought with quiet determination. "But what if we cannot walk all the way to the sun?"

"The sun is meant for no one," said Book, her voice firm as they approached a pair of widely spaced trees, interlocked by the braided twists of their branches. She sat clumsily beneath their shade. "I don't know how I will feel when we find it, and I don't know how I will feel if we do not."

Happy settled next to her, aching to explain how it was her legs and the suffocating possibility of being alone so worrying their golden eyes. How they could not help Book and would likely be stolen by sharpened teeth if her steps were ever to falter. How Happy was still getting used to the feeling of love.

"Have you noticed that things are looking different? The trees are lifting and colors have changed," said Book, startling Happy from their fogged worry. A gentle smile crested her swollen mouth as she observed the beating white flowers above them.

"Yes, well, seasons are shifting, and the forest rather enjoys it," replied Happy, following her gaze. It was not a good idea to worry over future words and forget to speak.

A creak of silence echoed as Book reached for her wilting rope.

"I do wonder why," she said, "I don't see change beyond the forest itself."

"Something must be happening we have not the privilege to see."

"Like what?" she asked, turning to her friend. "What do they see that we can't?" A sudden jolt of fear flashed across the resolved calmness of her face.

"Maybe it is a voice," Happy said. "Like the ones I used to have."

Book blinked, leaning back. "Where did they go?"

This was the first Happy had mentioned such an occurrence. They lay back, their scythe fastened against their stomach.

"I do not know, and I do not care to," Happy whispered, quietly resolute.

Book's hands fell from the noose. She rested her head upon the grass.

"Happy?" she said.

"Yes?"

"Have you ever missed them? The voices?"

Pale, snow-kissed flowers tilted their petals between the silence, blossoming so fully they soon tipped from leafy peaks and twirled with drowsy effervescence to the ground. Book, her inquiries seemingly forgotten, gazed toward the swirling, pixieish flowers.

Neither of them moved as stardust petals left their spots in the sky to dance through an invisible ballroom. For a brief while, the silvery shadows cast upon Happy's memory and the dark river trailing up Book's neck were lost in the calming mist of thought.

Not until the last ghostly petal had fallen did they rustle back into wakefulness. For Happy and Book had gone far away as the flowers drifted, lost in their own private imaginations. Happy stared at the scythe draped across their abdomen, turning it back and forth.

"No. No, I have not," they whispered.

12

A BIRCH TREE SONG

———

Glossy thoughts flashed beneath Happy's golden vision at the cool press of dawn. What would he think of such flowers? What would the twisted, fearful Man do if he knew of their quiet adoration of white petals?

"Are you ready for today's adventure?" asked Book, glancing at Happy. Still they lay beneath the embracing trees, allowing night to wash them upon its eventual morning shores.

"I am," Happy responded, looking away from her stiff legs. If anything, The Man could carry her.

Dizzied by a deep-rooted numbness sprouting from flower petals and bony fingers, Happy sat up, shaking their pointed head.

Book, propped against her elbows, studied Happy's troubled gaze and offered a disquieted smile.

Happy reminded themself that they'd only been gone for a short while on their red flower search. It cannot be possible to leave when you return. The Man would not come for them now. Not with Happy so defiantly set against him.

Placing her hands upon the damp earth, Book dragged her unbending legs forward until she rocked herself into a standing position. She did not wince. No, as pain was never held within her memory.

Happy, too, stood. The land ahead was marked by short, striking trees of pale bark and flowering branches.

Hardly had they begun walking before their nonsensical chatter latched upon one of a million noticeable things.

"Look at that tree, Happy," Book said, pointing with her short, dark fingers.

Gratefully drawn from their thoughts, Happy inspected a spindly trunk in front of them. "Yes, what about it?" they asked.

"It's white, like those flowers."

Memory snapped its whip.

"Why, that is a birch tree," Happy said.

It was thin and tall, a slight billowing mat of leaves sitting atop its callow frame.

"It's got black marks all across it," Book continued. "Why is that?"

Happy's voice thickened. "Perhaps from all the Times it woke up at night instead of day. The moon gave it a reminder to not forget again."

"I'm sure you are right. Sometimes trees can get forgetful." She examined Happy and their peering eyes.

"Do you remember The Man I told you of?" they asked, their distracted gaze wandering up the sapling's scrawny trunk.

Book's curious smile fell. She nodded.

"Yes, of course," she said, bitter. "He is the reason my name is Book rather than a bad name."

A strange, disconcerted feeling settled deep beneath Happy's glowing eyes. "Well, he told me that tree is a birch tree. They were his favorites."

Carelessly, they pointed with their scythe toward the young, ageless bark.

They never meant to touch it. Never wanted the tree to collapse.

Again. They had made another mistake.

***

Book, her mouth a tight press of fear, watched the tree sink, curling into a rotted mass before them. The forest yelped, sucking in a collective gasp; the sapling had been their child, and children are not meant to be taken so early. Then it was raining, and the pair was forced to walk onward.

"Happy?"

They did not respond, their gaze shielded by the pelting downpour.

Water dripped from a hanging leaf and onto Book's shoulder as puddling mud squelched beneath her toes. The gentle pattering reminded her of a long-ago when her own eyes had welled. The rain, however, was far more beautiful than such tears.

"Happy," she said again, holding a hand to the sky, "do you know what this rain sounds like?"

They glanced at her. "No. No, Book, I do not."

"It sounds like a song."

She had momentarily plucked at the strings of their curiosity. Happy lifted their sullen, drooping gaze. "What is that?"

She smiled. "It's hard to explain, but I guess you can compare it to love. But with a song, you feel it. Only once the song is over does the feeling leave. Unless you remember it later, of course. When you make your words sound like rain, you feel them more easily." She watched a droplet slide across her billowed jacket. "Your words can hold a different meaning than such words are meant to. Day can be night, happy can be sad; there is neither yes nor no, only the action of letting your feelings speak."

"A song certainly seems as complex as love."

Book's smile softened. "It does seem so, doesn't it?"

They walked on, both now fully aware of the pitter-pattering rainfall.

"Would you like to make one?" she asked as Happy's shoulders again slouched.

"Make what?"

"A song."

An excited bounce lifted their steps. "You can make one?"

"Of course!" she exclaimed, opening her hands. "We'll help each other."

The birch tree was ignored—but not forgotten—as Book and Happy became enraptured in the wonders of song making. There was no music, no tune, yet still, as Book began, it sounded just like water. Anciently innocent. Timeless yet new as an infant's touch.

We travel the forest trees
With no birds to guide us
No creatures to fear us
No branches to bide us
Just me, you and I, and the sun
We make choices and choose right
We feel good things and no fright
For it is just me, you and I, and the sun
Though Time dwindles further and Happy worries away
Though I understand little and Book walks slower each day
There will be me, you and I, and the sun!

And when we find it
What will happen then?
I do not know, but there still will be
Me and you and I

The night creatures fell silent, though Book and Happy had not spoken. Leaves forgot to rustle and the rain closed its watery curtain as the pair continued forward until the slender grass no longer sank with moisture. Book's rope was soaking and limp, her coat heavy. She became tired. A new feeling: exhaustion.

"Book," whispered Happy, their lantern gaze shining.

"Yes?"

"I think we should rest here."

"But there are no branches," she said, glancing at the shallow, grassy valley they'd stumbled across. Snaking bushes darted throughout the clearing, creating a holed wall against the surrounding birch trees. A single bent trunk curled from the ground, its leaves long departed and wooden limbs hollow and gray.

"There is no sunlight in darkness," Happy insisted.

"You're sure?"

"Of course."

And they lay upon the soaking, darkened grass.

***

As they sank into the muddied ground, Happy thought of their song, wondering if singing truthful words betrayed a definition. They studied Book's neck, a mixed array of ripe colors trailing beneath her mouth. Fearful their stare might solidify a reality they'd yet to understand, Happy averted their gaze from such swollen skin.

Instead, they turned to the sky, hoping stars would not shiver at their golden stare as the clouds whispered, conspiring to retake them. But Happy wanted Book to see them. To see the twinkling lights and not be afraid.

Next to them, Book gaped above, blinking without a cricket's interruption. She was too tired to smile, the soaked frills of her hair plastering her to the ground.

"Happy?" she whispered.

"Yes, Book?"

"What do you think the stars say to each other when it's quiet like now?"

Happy gazed at the rounded bump of Book's nose. "I do not know."

"Do they dance, Happy?" Her voice was a gasped murmur.

They peered above. "I think they must be dancing now."

Memory told them of a long-ago so deep in the past, even a few galaxies questioned its existence. A past in which Happy was surrounded by stars. Where they learned their first words and were told to not ask questions.

Watching Book, Happy remembered the two mistakes they'd made. Remembered how The Man's voice had sent their mind reeling.

But to call something a mistake does not necessarily mean it is bad.

They scanned the winking night.

"Do you think they like the quiet?" Happy asked, feeling a sudden outpouring of love.

"The stars?" Book replied.

"Yes."

"I am sure they do," she said after a moment's thought. "I am sure they talk about important things, and so need the quiet to think clearly."

"Book, do you think stars feel pain?"

She hesitated. "I'm not sure," she decided. "Sometimes I wonder if the feelings I feel are pain."

The outpouring warmth turned icy. "What do they feel like? Is it the rope or your skin?" Happy asked.

"No," she assured them. "I don't think so. It's just"—Book shrugged—"there are moments when I feel weaker."

"That is why we are resting." There came a tepid click of some wary insect.

"A different weakness," she insisted. "It thrums and aches. Oh, Happy, it's unpleasant, and I hope the stars don't feel the same."

"I think they are too far away to feel such things."

Book closed her eyes. For the rest of the night, Happy stared above them, tapping on the doors of Book's consciousness every so often. Never could they imagine such a feeling of loneliness.

13

CONSEQUENCES

———

Deep into night's slumber, Happy felt a nudge upon their hand. The soft, velvet petals.

"Book," they whispered, pulling their fingers away and stiffening, "the sunset flowers are back. The Man needs to see me." They sat up, rustling the forest's damp silence.

Book sharpened her sleepy frown. "Why do you need to, Happy? Why does he need you?" She sighed, immediately beaten.

"Well, he tells me things that I did not know before," said Happy, dunking their words into a pool of misguided sincerity. "He must teach me of the everything I do not yet understand."

Still without willpower to move, Book remained stubborn. "Why must you understand everything?"

"I do not know. Perhaps The Man will tell me." Happy stood as their shadowed limbs trilled with numbness. A blossoming trail poked through the moonlit brush. The creaking door of reason turned its lock.

Book shifted her head back, searching Happy's glazed lantern eyes. "I think he only wishes to teach you wrong things," she murmured, grasping her soaking rope. "Things that take you away until a night comes when you don't return."

A soft moment of compassion welled in Happy's clouded mind. "That will never happen, Book," they insisted.

She shook her head. "I think it may be too late for you to say that."

"I will ask him then," Happy continued. "Ask what he wishes to do."

"I'm not sure he will give you the right answer." A short breath of disappointment.

Happy turned to the red flower pathway. "I must try," they said, silencing the clanging reminder of what they last found at the trail's end. Those things The Man had tried to convince them of.

They began walking.

As Happy left the shallow valley, Book tugged at the noose around her neck, mumbling to herself.

"Sometimes I think you should just stay."

Happy allowed the automatic bend of their knees to carry them forward, stabbed with shame.

***

They were led to a sudden rise of earth, where runoff above splashed upon a jagged boulder jutting from the vertical mass of land. The Man sat folded upon the rock, a cave next to him, its mouth a dripping maw of moss and dampness. He looked up and smiled as Happy emerged from the thinning forest underbrush, their slouched form rising to meet bone-white teeth.

The Man waited for them to speak. The cave tapped his shoulder with moistened fingertips, slurring groans echoing throughout its darkened chambers. What must live there, to sound so completely lost?

Happy stared. The Man's sunken eyes were blurred, blank pools.

"I did something wrong," they said finally, head bowed.

The Man tilted his head. "Did you?"

"Yes. The tree. I took a birch sapling."

The Man stood, approaching Happy with quietly sinister footsteps. His pointed smile curled with the sweet twinge of satisfaction. Happy forced themself to stand still.

"Now isn't that familiar?" he said, circling Happy, his head just reaching those towering shoulders. "I thought for once I might have taught you something, but your inabilities seem only to grow in number."

"It was—"

"A mistake? Oh, you have made many of those recently. Can you fix the irreversible?"

"No."

"Then why do you tell me these things? What do you gain from this?" The Man grabbed Happy's scythe, pulled it from behind their back. "Does it make you feel better, to think your ever-increasing sins might be lessened?" He ran a finger across the bladed end. Leaned up toward pulsing eyes. "Well, let me *enlighten* you. I don't feel sympathy, foolish Creature."

The Man dropped Happy's hand and stalked toward the cave's drooling entrance, his grin disappearing.

"So that I may learn how to fix it," Happy said, their arms hanging limply.

The Man whirled around, the cavernous abyss behind him blanching his already pale frame.

"Can you become any more ignorant?" he yelled across the distance. "Are you incapable of understanding what it means to listen? You have no willingness to pay attention.

You only *destroy*! Did you hear that? Did that break into your mind?" The Man took a breath and pointed at the cave. "I want you to walk until you use your hands to guide you."

Happy went rigid. "I cannot do that."

"Why?"

"I may touch something."

"Well, you lost the privilege of worrying about that, haven't you?" The Man pulled dry air into a depthless laugh. "You have abandoned everything but frivolous desire, so don't entertain me with beliefs of regret. I am letting you do what it is you seem determined to accomplish."

"I never wish to hurt anything."

"Walk, or the number of things you've wished for will rise from the ground and pull you in with their stench of decay."

Happy considered their webbed feet, slowly forcing them to move. Muddy grass fell to stone and clouded moonlight was replaced with a sudden, condensing weight. A suffocating pressure without direction or destination.

That wretched, drawling cavern cry might soon burst from Happy, and they did not like that thought as they walked into the cave, the glow of their eyes dulled by an engulfing darkness. Their hands soon twitched, palms begging to open.

They stumbled at a sudden, rocky decline, managing to restrain the frantic tug of their arms. Book and her tearfully resigned words—the lines of her frown—ultimately stopped them.

Happy had not listened to their friend. Ignored her fears and the understanding that they'd caused them.

So Happy did not make it far. Did not grasp whatever lesson The Man was trying to teach them, because Book lay in the draining night not so far away. And she felt alone when she was not, and walked when she shouldn't. What it must now be like to truly have no one to talk to?

Guilt is a terrible thing, but it spurred Happy to turn around, carefully reversing the steps they'd already committed. They stalled at the cave's crooked-mouth opening.

The Man, at his place upon the jagged rock, showed no emotion beyond a clenched jaw. Happy felt the bitter taste of failure. The burn of resentment.

"Why do you do this?" they asked, averting their pulsing gaze.

Dawn silhouetted The Man's thin, almost sickly body. He sighed. "Again with the questions," he said, voice slow with exhaustion. "Do you really want to know the answer?"

Happy remained silent.

"Because I like to, you poor creature. You need this. To be reminded of the millions of things you pretend don't exist."

"I do not think that."

"Oh yes. I forget that ignorance justifies all those things you've done. Tell me, do you call such actions *mistakes* to idolize whatever fantasy you've run away with?"

"I know I have done wrong things," Happy insisted weakly.

The Man waited for a nonexistent excuse. "You have not made mistakes," he said finally, "but choices. I have already presented you with many solutions. It was you who decided. You who allowed for such ends."

He waved a hand. A dismissal.

"Leave."

As Happy dragged themself back into the trees and dewy shadows, they realized they had forgotten to ask about The Man's intentions.

They tripped over a rock.

Perhaps Book was right. He would not have answered.

14

THE BIRCH TREE

———

A Summer Long-Ago:

They walked together, he and the Creature, brush shying back into the ground as a parched heat sucked moisture from their stems. The Creature wanted to ask where they were going and why The Man carried a rope in his hands. The trees were smaller here, and It didn't like how large It felt surrounded by little things.

After a silent march, The Man, weaving thick vines up his legs, spoke in a quiet voice.

"I have not seen you in a while."

The Creature knew this voice. Knew It was about to learn something new.

"Yes," responded the Creature.

"I have been traveling. The world is much larger than what your eyes may see."

"Yes, I remember."

"But you often forget," The Man growled. "What happens when you forget things?"

"The world may crumble."

"Not just the world."

"Everything."

This day was cloudy. Always cloudy when the Creature ventured far.

"You do not know everything," continued The Man, jostling the rope.

"Yes."

"So how could you possibly know that everything may crumble?"

"Because you say so."

The Man sniffed. "You are going to learn something new today," he said. "Just one of the innumerable things your frail mind obscures."

They arrived at a clearing, where brush hung lean and sour. In the center, a sapling no taller than the Creature Itself frolicked and danced with broad, flapping leaves. The Man smiled as they approached, and the tree went still.

With thin fingers, he caressed its pale wood, thumbing black scars scattered across its trunk.

The Creature watched, trying hard to keep a blank mind.

"Get on your knees," The Man said, and the Creature obeyed. "Give me your hands." And the Creature did so.

The Man's smile never faltered, but grew until his needle teeth glared against the dusty sky. He grabbed the Creature and tied Its pitch-black wrists around the sapling. Rope was a new feeling for the Creature, soft and rigid. The scythe hung awkwardly toward The Man as he stepped back, just in front of the Creature and Its bound hands. Those broad leaves no longer danced, but trembled.

"Do you know what this is?" He pointed to the tree.

"It is a tree."

"No, it is not." He snapped, the tree dying so suddenly, it took the Creature a moment to realize it was because of Its own ill-spoken words. Silent, silent, silent—the feeling of guilt and failure.

"What is this?" The Man said, voice rising.

"I do not know."

"You fool!" A snap, and the tree died. Almost flippantly, it was reborn, frail trunk heaving between the Creature's hands. "What is this?" he shouted, glaring at the Creature. "What is this thing in front of you? Tell me, or I fear the world may collapse."

"Please! I am sorry, but I do not know! Please do not let everything crumble." The tree died. Again. And again it was reborn.

"You coward!" The Man yelled, laughing. "You absolute coward! To beg. You think me all-knowing. You think me brimming with truth, yet I cannot even teach you a simple word you already know. What is it?"

"It is a tree! It is a tree within my hands." Dead. Dead and alive.

"Useless! Hands are useless if you do not know what is between them."

The Man paced around the Creature, rubbing his palms together, face gaunt. The Creature felt a million things. How could It not know? How could It not know this simple thing? Because if this one simple thing was not known, the tree would again die.

But it is not a tree. But it will die.

It would die, and the feelings-that-were-not-Its-feelings had said nothing to tell It the tree was empty of Time.

Too many thoughts. Too many thoughts inside the Creature's unblinking eyes as The Man paced and grew the tree again.

"What will happen if you do not know?" The Man asked, standing again in front of limp wrists.

"Everything will crumble."

It hurt to know this.

"Then what is this?" he asked again. "What is this one tiny bit of the everything you claim to protect?"

"I do not—"

"Don't you say those words!"

The Creature watched it die again. Fall and reform. The tree's black slashes pushed against dark hands as the defeated Creature hung Its finned head. Then, those feelings spoke to It. Barely could the words escape Its thoughts. The poor being, kneeling in the dirt, had never felt so weighed down by existence.

"It is a birch tree," It whispered.

Still it died.

***

Slowly, The Man allowed bark to reform, its limbs curling and haggard. He peered at the Creature now as those golden eyes rose toward his own.

"You will not leave until that tree is soaked like rain into the ground. Do you understand?" he said.

"Yes."

"And what is its name?"

"It is a birch tree."

The Man left the Creature there, folded and tied upon the ground. He shook off the remnants of dirt and simply walked away. Yet he heard it. He heard the slow march of decay as leaves fell and bark caved to maggots and endings. A dreaded feeling hung chains along his stomach, and The Man's smile slipped away quietly as he, without glancing back, made the tree grow again.

15

COMPLICATIONS

———

"What's he like?" Book asked the next morning as they crossed a trickling forest creek, her voice careful as she toed a stick at the water's edge. Watched it flow downstream.

"Who?" Happy responded as the stick bumped into streaming, long-stemmed plants.

"Well, Happy, who else would it be? I cannot speak of many people."

How do you make clear the silhouette of one so shrouded in their own confusion?

"Yes, of course." Happy began walking across the shallow, bitingly cold water, the flow halting at their touch. "He is complicated."

"Love can be complicated, but I don't think The Man is like love," said Book, planting her stiff legs upon a protruding rock behind Happy.

"No," Happy agreed hesitantly, "he is not like love, but he is hard to explain."

Book caught the nervous twitch of Happy's fingers. "Why?" she asked.

"Because I have never had someone to talk with before."

"Anyone beside him."

"Yes," said Happy. They glanced back at Book. "I think it might have been his voice. Perhaps he lived in my head completely."

Book swung a leg forward.

"That couldn't have been nice," she responded, gruff with barely concealed frustration.

"No. I do not think it was."

"So he's bad," Book said.

"He is burdened."

As she staggered to another rock, Book stared wide-eyed at her friend.

"How can he be burdened when it is you that must touch things and watch them fall?" she asked, her words drained of any lingering vexation.

Happy reached the stream's end and water sighed back into its instinctive flow. Their answer came automatically, a repeated line instilled by infinite sunrises.

"Because The Man knows of everything," they said.

"I thought he was to teach you of that?"

"He will, as it is bigger than even the sun." A poisoned tone of reverence. "Than the stars and all the skies that hold them."

"I am sure that cannot be a pleasant thing to bear," Book said tentatively, rocking her legs until she managed to stand beside Happy. "But he has hurt you."

"I am not injured, Book."

"Yes, but I see how your eyes shake when water stills. I have not forgotten the pond you once lived in."

Rugged, mottled trees crowded before them, their branches rippling waves of green. Happy gazed ahead, shaking their head. "He said I must do what I am told. Everything might collapse if I do not listen."

"But Happy," Book said, pulling their golden eyes downward, "we have walked for a long while, and nothing has changed but the ground we rest upon."

Happy poked a curl of Book's dark hair. "You are right," they said. "Maybe The Man meant something different."

"Maybe he is just wrong. Maybe the right words for what he knew of didn't exist when you met him." Book crossed her arms, frowning.

The two continued their trek through the forest as dawn light spattered itself through thick, draping branches.

"He made me, Book," Happy whispered, glancing at their midnight scythe. "I never met him, as he is all I have ever known."

Book glared forward. "That sounds almost worse than stalled water."

Happy nearly tripped. "Why is that?" they asked.

"Because, Happy, you say The Man is hard to explain. That you were never given a chance to judge him." She grabbed at her noose, tugging at its end. "But I think there's less than what you're imagining."

"What do you mean?"

Could a million lifetimes be so simplified?

Book paused, scrounging her words together. "He speaks in your head with a voice you did not wish for," she said.

"Yes."

"He made you live alone in water that was dark and murky."

"That is true, Book," Happy said, their steps slowing.

"And he tells you of this 'everything' that is impossible to understand," Book continued, her gaze sparking. "That its existence depends upon what you do."

Happy nodded, their mind pulled in opposite directions.

"Yet you left. You *left*, Happy, and nothing has happened. And I don't think anything will."

"But there is much he cannot explain," Happy said feebly.

"Yet he sends for you with sunset flowers," Book continued, her voice hardening. "He isn't telling you to come, but asking."

"How might that determine his character?"

"He has shown that you can make choices, Happy, where before he decided them for you." Book's eyes were lit beneath the black stain of her irises. "He is a secretive Man."

"But he knows of everything," Happy repeated quietly.

"A lie is hard to spot if that is all you are ever told," said Book, eyeing a berry-covered bush ahead of them. "I will believe what I know."

They walked in silence for a while, ducking beneath branches and pretending the leafy whispers did not bother them. Pale flowers speckled the ground.

"He is not terrible," Happy whispered, but even the trees could hear the doubt in their voice.

Book caught a glimpse of those wide lantern eyes. "Is that what you know?" she asked.

Happy turned their scythe, the bladed end dipping and raising like a dark wave.

"It is what I imagine," they said finally.

***

They walked deep into the night, until spindled trees warped into rooted masses at a sharp, shadowy incline of rock and thickened grass. Book's legs began trembling.

"We must stop, Book," Happy whispered gently.

Book waved a hand. "My legs don't care for rest," she said. "It'll only be worse tomorrow."

"Well, we cannot try tonight." Happy looked around, spotting a log thrown behind a pair of shriveled thickets, surrounded by rock. They pointed. "We can stay there while we wait."

"What can we wait for, Happy? I cannot be fixed." Book dragged herself toward the flaking lump of wood, teetering with every footstep.

"I do not know," said Happy, walking behind her, "but The Man once told me that hills only get steeper."

She huffed. "Then we'll be stuck here."

"You also told me you are not patient, so I do not think that can happen either."

Book offered a grudging smile, dust pluming as she dropped to the ground. Happy sat across from her, pulling their legs in close. The air was still and humid, devoid of a breeze to jostle the nighttime coolness.

Happy wondered where the wind had gone, its breathy sighs once companion to Book's hanging feet. Her feet that could no longer tilt upward, poking through the baggy ends of her jeans. She now picked at the muddy clumps sprinkled around her, watching the dirt run from her fingers like stained raindrops.

"What do you think we will see when we reach the hill's end?" asked Happy, copying Book and scooping a dreary piece of earth.

She set her eyes on them, quirking her mouth in thought. "I'm not sure. Perhaps we can make up a story of what we might find," she said.

"A story?" The dirt fell from their long, uncurled fingers.

"Perhaps you should tell one."

"What is told in a story?"

"Anything," Book said as Happy leaned back, shocked by the infinity of storytelling. They gazed out into the forest spreading just below them, feeling The Man's nagging claim of *everything*. How had Book simply condensed it into a single breath of eternities?

"How do you tell one?" they asked.

Book wiped her fingers upon her jeans. "With words, of course."

Again the aching tug of excitement and worry. If *everything* is impossible to explain, then how might it be so easily told?

"It can be a story of what has already happened," she continued, "or begin to exist as you speak it. It can even be both at the same Time. A story is like the sky, Happy."

"How so?"

"You say a story, and it lives forever like the sky does."

"Can they really last that long?"

"Yes. Because stars burn and dwindle," Book said and dropped another clump of dirt, "the earth crumbles beneath our hands, but the sky is way above us. So high up, I think the sun cannot reach it. Stories last as long as the sky, because the sky will last forever."

Happy felt complexity's thread unwind into a thin line of understanding.

"And if no one looks up at it?" they asked, gazing toward the masked night.

"The sky will never know. It is too far away to hear our thoughts or words."

Happy studied her. "And you want me to tell one?"

Book let her hands fall to her lap. "If you'd like to," she said.

Happy flexed their tendrilled fingers, the scythe bursting from their wrist. They wondered why The Man had never dared tell them a story. Did not like the reasoning as to why.

"Of course, but I will be needing help, Book. The Man never taught me of stories."

"I don't think he wished you to know of them."

Happy sprinkled dirt upon the ground, nodding solemnly. "I think you are right."

The forest crackled in the brief moment of silence, festering in a conjured, lukewarm apprehension.

What will they say?

"This is the story of the wind," began Happy, leaning forward. "The wind that has never joined us on our journey but always runs just ahead."

Book grinned, her broken, decaying legs forgotten in the twinkle of her eyes.

"The wind tripped and fell over itself, as it had forgotten how to walk," Happy continued. "One day, as it sprinted across a treeless field, an emerging shadow made the wind halt, right there in the grass. This shadow did not move when the wind shoved it but remained still upon the ground." Happy paused and asked, "Am I telling the story correctly?"

"There is no wrong way. Keep going."

"Why aren't you moving?" asked the wind.

"Because I come from a place that you cannot touch," replied the shadow. "Why do you run?"

The wind, after perhaps a million, million years without pausing for breath, sat upon the ground, next to the stagnant shadow.

"Because I must," they said in an exhausted sort of way.

"Would you like to do something else?" asked the shadow with a dark voice, suddenly grabbing the wind's shoulders and dragging them into a world without grass to rustle or trees or animals. It was a world of shadow. There were no shapes and no light.

"This is not what the wind wanted, a world so confusing it was impossible to make choices. As soon as the shadow entered this empty land, the wind turned back. "I need to leave," they said.

The shadow became upset, as they were now in its land. Bitterness climbed into its throat and the shadow screamed, "I brought you to a place that will not tire you with obligation! Why do you reject spending even a moment within it?" It opened its mouth then, showing the wind a staircase of stars, leading to even greater, swirling darkness.

"You never let me answer. I was not given a choice," the wind shouted back. "I did not ask for an escape, but company." The shadow didn't get a chance to grab at the wind's shifting arms as they leapt as high as they could go, high enough to pull themself back onto earth by the trembling ends of grass.

"They jumped to their feet and looked around, back in the now still field. No one asked for the wind to run again. Not the grass or the trees or the bushes. It was quiet, without a single expectation but the mere hope of existence. So the wind walked, brushing the forest instead of shaking its branches, and renamed itself the breeze."

Attentive brown trees waited for the girl's reaction, their branches taut. Why had the being's words seemed so kind?

Book leaned against the log, stretching her hands out until joints cracked all along her arms.

"That was a lovely story, Happy," she whispered, her words puffed with adoration.

"Was it?" Happy asked, clasping their hands together. It had not seemed as difficult as The Man had made it out to be.

"I think so. It made me feel"—she met Happy's eyes, widening her outstretched arms—"like I could be bigger than I am now. Like I could come back from the shadow world if I remembered what the wind once did."

Happy lay back and reached toward the cloudy night sky. "Thank you, Book."

"Of course."

"And we will think of something," Happy insisted. "We will climb the hill or walk around it, or maybe the creek knows a shortcut."

The ends of Book's smile dribbled with a faint, hopeless sadness.

"Maybe."

***

Long before the skies could lighten, a sunset flower blossomed next to Happy's wrist. They watched its petals twirl into existence, revolving around that pitch-black center.

A battle played within their captured mind as they stood, murmuring a few distracted words to their friend, whose decaying mouth deepened into an empty-cave frown of abandonment.

Happy thought of stories. Of the *everything* The Man said could never be explained. The questions they'd never dared to ask. And as they laid their webbed feet toward the red, glowing trail, Happy assured themself of the need to know. The answers they'd never believed themself worthy of.

Oh, but they had forgotten about those feelings. Those words that were not their own. How they once whirred like a second consciousness. A numb, tranquilizing rush suppressed Happy's weakened thoughts.

Your mind is poisoned. Are you really so corrupted as to think yourself deserving?

They oozed into Happy's mind until their footsteps were no longer controlled by intention. The task of asking was thrown into a boiling pit the voice had dragged along with it.

That's right. Come to me.

Flowers led the being beneath darkened canopies.

The girl could not walk, and was left alone.

16

MEETING TIME

Happy had never looked at anything so intently. The flowers swayed their scarlet petals, seeming to revolve around their black-hole centers. Painfully beautiful within the thick forest shadows. Happy followed their red pathway, hardly noticing the forest recoil at their whispered touches across a tree trunk or a misstep upon sprouting grass. They stepped across the creek, blind to whatever memories had just been made there.

They had never been reckless before. Uncaring. The forest, so fearful of Happy and their mind of hesitation, now watched as their thoughts eroded with unknown intention.

Upon rounding a rusted oak tree, Happy's gaze collided with a pair of eyes staring straight back at them. Pupils of stained leather pushed deep beneath thick, lake-green skin. A thing. A living thing that was not running away but a solid presence within Happy's pinhole line of sight. Behind a wrinkled, earless head rose a shell that seemed carved from a mountaintop, immense and rugged. The ghost of memory.

Tortoise.

She watched Happy straighten into a taut pole of fear, the wrinkled line of her mouth lifting into a smirk. Those golden eyes searched desperately for an escape, a path without ancient, breathing things. The voice had gone silent.

Then she smiled a toothless grin and began talking with a voice not heard but felt, just like Book's.

"I suppose I should speak first, seeing as I've crossed your path."

Happy did not answer, shocked.

"Perhaps it is strange that I'm speaking to you," she continued, eyes twinkling. "Everyone else is afraid of you, I know." Happy stood still as the tortoise cocked her head, deep wrinkles folding as she moved. Her snubbed nose lifted, mouth a gouged river of cracks. "Yes, this has not happened to you before. I'm alive." She snorted. "Well, barely."

"Why?" Happy managed, looking away from her.

"Why what? Don't get stumped by a single word. We both know thoughts aren't that childish."

"Why are you talking to me?"

The tortoise, sinking back onto impossibly worn feet, emitted a slow and hollow sigh. Her entire body seemed in a constant ripple, straining each thick layer of skin and reacting to a movement made an entire lifetime ago. "Because I have watched you all my life," she said, "and whatever expression that laced across your face was one I'd never seen before. I cannot say it was a comforting look. Rather unsettling, actually."

"But you move slowly. Surely I walk faster than all four of your legs," Happy said, caught by curiosity.

"That might be understood without explanation."

"Yes, but—"

"And where were you going?"

The tortoise hardly moved save for her massive head, which bobbed ever so slowly.

"I am going to see The Man," said Happy. "He calls for me with red flowers." She was much bigger than Book. Book and her weak, decaying legs.

"And why must you answer?" inquired the tortoise.

"I always have."

"Yes. And did this friend of yours exist in that portion of always?"

Happy hesitated. "How do you know of my friend?"

The tortoise clicked her beak-like mouth. "For what other reason would you have left that pond?"

A breath of silence eased between them as Happy stumbled for words. Book would not like a living thing speaking of her. They could imagine her grabbing the frayed end of her rope and pressing it close.

"Do you know him? The Man?" they said finally.

She sighed, her confidence momentarily shaken. "It is impossible not to notice whenever he is near. Leaves and branches and stems grow in a quick, choking sort of way."

Again, Happy did not answer. Why would a living thing push against growth?

"Yes, you are confused," the tortoise continued, eyes watering with humor. "Perhaps if you imagine someone sending you farther into darkness, you'd better understand."

"Darkness is the opposite of life," Happy replied, overcome by their curiosity.

"For you, they are quite similar. Darkness is the direction your existence leads, is it not?"

The pond. Happy did not want to remember the murky blankness that was still water.

"And so," the tortoise continued, "you don't strive to be pushed toward darkness. I see the same thing with the leaves and trees. They are forced out of their own lives and into the will of The Man."

"I am sure he does not mean to hurt them," said Happy, studying their palms.

"And I am not so sure you believe that."

Happy was unsure whether they wanted to leave or continue talking to the tortoise blocking their path. And though they had begun speaking of The Man and his flowers, Happy could no longer remember why it had seemed so important to follow them. To learn some painful lesson.

"Have you ever spoken to him?" Happy asked, as they couldn't think of anything else worth saying.

"I wouldn't dare to."

"Why is that?"

She again snorted. "Do you mean to tell me you have no fear? You poor thing. I've seen you for thousands of sunrises, and never have those eyes squeezed themselves into anger. But your hands. I have seen them shake."

Again, Happy fell quiet. They did not like how fear made them think of Book and her staggering steps.

The tortoise waited, harnessing a secret, calming knowledge Happy could not understand. The Man became a slurred thought, overwhelmed by Book's bleeding, crooked feet.

They walked so much. Every day they step-stepped until no light remained to see by. Happy glanced at their scythe before meeting the tortoise's gaze.

"What is your name?" Happy spoke before they could imagine what Book would say of such a rash idea.

The tortoise's deep-seated eyes shone. "Why do you assume I have one?" she asked, amused.

"Well, I must call you something. Book told me I made her Happy, and so that is my name. Books are stories that last beyond memory, and so that is hers."

"Yes, I see now," she said with another click of her beak. "You can call me Time."

Happy shifted their webbed feet. "Would you like to travel with us, Time? Book has legs that do not listen and feet that go in wrong directions. You are much larger than she is, and you have a shell that is solid and hard." They paused for a moment, meeting those black eyes. "Would you carry her? Would you carry my friend so that we may find the sun?"

Time did not look away as she answered. "Of course, you poor thing. I will join you."

Happy felt the relieved warmth of a smile. They turned and began leading Time back through the trees, toward Book and their search for the sun.

***

Happy did not notice The Man watching from behind a barrel-chested oak tree, overcome by the roaring thunder of excitement. Yet Time, in her thousands of sunrises, knew the feeling of hatred, and glanced back at him, ancient patience disguising her slowness. One, two, three breaths passed as she simply observed the flower-sprouting human. After a moment, The Man turned and stalked away.

17

BOOK'S ENCOUNTER

———

Happy appeared suddenly from the haggard wall of brush, swirling chambers of darkness drenching their spindly form.

The refreshment of company wiped away Book's wretched thoughts of being alone.

"I am back," said Happy, excitedly clasping and releasing their hands.

"Why so quickly?" she asked, jerking her head up. Hopeful. "Was The Man not there?"

"I did not find out. Someone stopped me from walking."

"Someone?" Her stomach lurched.

"I met someone, and they gave me good advice. Remember how you cannot walk very far, Book? How your legs are stiff and crumpled?"

Book slumped back upon the rotting stump. "Yes, I've never forgotten."

"Well, I have been nervous for the day they stop working, as we could no longer continue our journey."

"You can carry me, Happy," Book mumbled, shrugging. "I'm not afraid."

"Yes, but I am worried I will hurt you. That I will make a mistake and send you into a place from which you cannot return like I do with forest things."

"I trust you."

"But we do not have to worry about that now," Happy insisted, almost frantic. "I have found someone who will help us."

"Then where are they?" Book glanced around, suspicion clogging her strangled throat.

"She said I should warn you of her entrance," continued Happy, looking behind them. "Give you a moment to process the change."

"What change? Happy, I don't like this. This is our adventure. We have never needed anyone else."

"But we will. Book, I know you can hear the crack of your knees when you are forced to bend them."

"I need no one else but you."

"She will help us. It will be easier to continue," Happy said softly. They glanced behind them.

Book watched the nervous flick of golden eyes. "What's her name? What is she like?"

"She is kind. A quiet, patient kind of intelligence."

"She is not like me," she said, lips wobbling.

"No, I am not," said the something, stepping out from the shield of forest brush.

Book's mouth fell open, stopped only by the puffy swell of her neck.

A tortoise, her shell equal in height to Happy's chest, peered forward, neck long and stretched. Her peeking eyes twinkled and the box of her head ended in a snub-nosed point. She was lined heavily in wrinkles, and buried within them, a perpetual grin opened.

Book remained stunned in terror.

"My name is Time," continued the tortoise, her voice creaking like wood.

Happy glanced between them, clasping their slender hands together.

"Book, I know this is not an expected thing—"

"She's living, Happy!" Book managed, her raised brows disappearing beneath the wreath of her hair. She dragged her eyes from Time, still attempting to register her spoken, intentional words.

"I am also a tortoise," said Time before Happy could respond. "I am many things, but it would be past sunrise before we listed them all."

Book turned back to her, narrowing her milky stare. "Who are you?" she questioned, the slightest waver to her words. She pushed at her legs, begging them to move.

"Did I not just answer that?" Time said and chuckled, tilting her head.

Again, Book gaped. Happy went to stand next to her, leaning down as Book reached deftly for her rope.

"I know this is scary," Happy whispered, "but she is not like the others we have met. She is not like the fluffy-tailed creature or the trees."

"You don't know someone by judging one conversation," Book hissed, whirling her head to meet nervous golden eyes. Her hair bounded after her, feet stagnated.

Happy pulled away slightly. "Perhaps, but I do not think we get the privilege of waiting for history's purity to make itself clear."

Book huffed and glanced at the tortoise. She had yet to move, watching the two of them with a distanced interest.

"What do you want?" Book asked, ignoring whatever attempt Happy was making at persuasion, nearly scrambling away as Time stepped forward.

"What a question, really," she said, her nubbed toes crunching against the dusk-tinged earth, "as you would never believe I genuinely want to help you. No, that is not an answer I think you'd accept, no matter my sincerity." The tortoise sniffed and dipped her head toward Book. "What if I told you that I have seen your friend before? That I've seen the pond from which they come?"

Book refused to look away, her little hands clenched tightly.

"And what if I told you I stood by, watching this being lurk through the shadows, believing the trees' claim that It meant to impale us with a sword cut from night skies? Its slouched frame clinging to the darkness as if to better elude our fearful gazes?"

She took another step as Book ground her teeth in frustration. "I never did anything to challenge that thought. Not until the ages blurred together and forest things eventually fell to Happy's touch, only for newer saplings to replace them. Only then I allowed myself to ask: When had I ever seen this being, its eyes said to be stolen rays of sunshine, harm the living? Even when It caused entire canopies to fall, It did so only when their branches were stripped bare by countless winters."

The tortoise regarded Happy for a brief moment, wincing against an ancient shame. "So, Book, I want to help you for all those moments I glimpsed your friend hiding in the brush and merely turned away as forest trees screamed at them. Because I cannot bear to ignore the lies any longer."

Book twisted a loose strand of rope around her finger. Blinked the drooling pools of her eyes.

"I don't know you," Book said, leaning daringly forward and pointing at Time's beaked nose, "and after one conversation, I have not changed my mind. Happy and I don't belong anywhere except with each other, and you will take that away.

I will touch your skin, ride upon your shell, but I want you to know that you are not welcome. You are a mere tool we are forced to use."

The tortoise smiled that wide-wrinkled grin. "Then there are many more conversations to come."

Book did not respond but turned to Happy. "Perhaps we should go now."

18

UP THE HILL

———

Climbing upon the tortoise's jaded shell was humiliating. The subdued morning gazed on warily as Book swung a bare foot upon the base of Time's neck, the skin shockingly fluid beneath her fingers.

As Time lifted her head, Book rose until the shell's peak straddled her vision and she bumped into its shore-like base, grasping the cracked, muddy-green surface. She forced herself to crawl forward, until the sloping rock evened and she turned, if only to see what adventures might come forward.

Her small, dirt-crusted hands shook as the tortoise stood. Book did not like feeling a heartbeat so close to her, and tears dragged across her grime-spattered face.

"Are you alright, Book?" said Happy, just in front of Time. Still, they towered above her, Book's lifted eyes just below her friend's shoulders.

She sniffed, glancing out at the forest. "Yes."

"I know this must be difficult." Happy's voice was soft.

Book shrugged. "Perhaps, but we must find the sun."

"Alright."

Happy turned, shifting to the side as Time lumbered a few steps up the hill's rocky surface. Coiled, sharpened brush seemed now fully illuminated from Book's spot above them. What was once a single tooth became a yawning mouth of fangs, munching at the brown earth. The previous opening between thin, lean trees rose into scraggly barricades of branches. Still air passed unwillingly across Book's feet, and she grabbed for the rope. Time paused, glancing back.

"Are we steady?" she asked, her words lifted by sincerity.

"I'm fine," Book mumbled, peering into those needle eyes.

Time continued on, Happy next to her, trees thinning around them until the gray dawn sky blossomed with curving orchestras of gathered clouds.

Four legs, and Book could feel each independent step halt to allow another's passage. Four working legs with joints that didn't pop or swell a little more each day.

"What made you decide to travel with us?" Book asked as Time slowly dodged a thorny tangle of brambles.

"It was no decision. Your friend invited me."

"Your legs are much shorter than Happy's."

The tortoise's wrinkled grin rose and faced her. "Short legs do not make for missed opportunities."

"If you had my legs," continued Book, "you never would have met them, and my legs are shorter than yours."

"Perhaps that is true."

"It's working legs that give you such good things."

Happy walked in silence, rubbing their hands together and flickering lantern eyes toward Book. She wore a frothy mask of desperation, straining for Happy to see clearly. To see how a girl with a rope around her neck should not be riding upon the shell of Time.

"We're different from you," said Book, watching as the slanted brush bumbled across her jostling vision. "The living think we're bad."

Happy's pittering eyes held still. "We are not bad, Book," they interrupted quietly.

Book looked away, squinting at the rugged, leveling incline. "I'm finding it harder to believe that. I used my feet for only so many days before the forest took them away from me."

"That could not have been the forest," Happy said. "They wouldn't dare touch us."

"What could it be, then?" whined Book, shaking her head. "There was nothing else but you and me."

Happy glanced at the thickened grasses fighting against the toughened ground. "Perhaps when I brought you back, I did not do it exactly right," they whispered.

"We are not living things. We were never meant to be right," Book said, glaring at her hands pressed upon Time's shell.

"That cannot be true."

Time's head dipped with each ancient step.

"If only I were walking," Book mumbled.

***

When they made it upon the hill's opposite end, dusk sauntering warily into view, Time broke the steeping silence. Trees again rose, their limp-wristed branches hanging from knotted trunks, quite unlike the previous forest. They loomed darkly, imperious and forlorn.

"I am a tortoise, as you both know," said Time, trekking behind Happy and their carefully placed footsteps. "I am a living thing, yet another obvious fact. But, and here, Book, I'd like you to understand, I am innumerable levels of imperfect. I walk slow, my legs are thick and cannot climb. My teeth are flat, and many cracks travel across my shell, which is too light in color to properly hide me in the brush. What superiority does life grant me?

Book did not answer, peering into the rounded night shadows.

"I need rest, yet whenever I awaken, exhaustion has not left me," the tortoise continued. "I am not like you, but to deny me my impurity is simply wrong. Tell me, does comparing yourself to the forest cure whatever misgivings you hold?"

"I don't have misgivings," Book replied.

Happy's head bowed low against their shoulders.

"You certainly hold something," Time said. "I can feel it dragging at those arms, pushing itself upon my shell."

Book grabbed at her swollen cheeks and shouted, anger's leather whip catching her hand as she vomited noise.

"You don't know me!" she cried. "My flaws aren't something you get to name."

Time rattled a breath, her steps now hesitant as leaning canopies watched. "I was not trying to name," she said, "but to understand."

"Yet you won't listen."

"I listen and respond. Interpret and wonder."

Book simmered quietly, sifting through her sandy emotions and fumbling with the word *listen*. The coils of her hair brushed against a low-hanging branch, and she flinched.

"Truly, I am sorry if I appear insensitive," Time continued, chuckling, "but many seasons have passed since another has heard my voice. Perhaps I have forgotten that with response comes reaction." She gazed at Happy, whose head lifted, and said, "Fear lives in all of us, and I merely want you to know this. To know that I have always been scared."

In a breath of weakness, Book asked, "What are you afraid of?"

Time sighed. "I wish it were a simple answer."

The tortoise, being, and girl fell silent as night swept them into its river. Trees pushed against the hazy starlight, stretching their branches as clicking creatures sang deep within their leaves.

After Time inquired about rest, they settled upon the ground, patched with soft dirt and budding grass. Book slid from Time's shell, leaning upon the tortoise's side as her arms itched too much to endure crawling. Happy lay down in front of them, their pulsing eyes flicking toward the nervous twitch of Book's fingers.

Darkness crept forward, and the tortoise slept.

19

PAST THINGS

———

Just before dawn, when dreamy purples still tinted the air, Time awoke, shifting the massive rock of her head until she faced Happy, whose pulsing eyes pointed to the clustered leaves above.

"Tell me," the tortoise said as Happy looked at her, "what circumstance caused you to leave?"

"To leave?"

"To leave that pond of glass."

"I—" Happy glanced at Book slumped upon Time's shell, ice pouring across their chest. "I made a friend, and friends are not meant to be apart from one another."

Time nodded. "That is true," she said, her eyes twinkling. "Would you believe me, Happy, if I told you I've never had a friend?"

"I do not think you are lying."

"Without anyone to share it with, life can be a lonely thing."

Happy clasped their hands together as pale fingers and sharp teeth flashed across their memory.

"I am sorry," they said finally. "Perhaps one day you could become Book's and my friend."

"Really?" Time smiled, her wrinkles groaning.

"Book once told me of love. How it is warm and steady. How it can beat cold. We have not known you very long, and maybe love will find us."

The hushed tremor of night sat between them.

"She is a sharp thing," Time pondered after a moment.

Happy again gazed at frilled curls as Book remained stubbornly silent.

"You see her edges, as that is all she believes you want to find," they said, turning back to the tortoise.

Time smacked her beaked mouth somberly.

"Yes," she said, "I can understand that." Pausing, she studied the golden framework of Happy's eyes, as if picking at the nerves piecing them together. "Thank you."

Happy nodded. "Of course."

Time tilted her gaze, searching. "And what of The Man?" she asked. "Do you love him?"

The beam of assurance no longer held their automatic answer.

"I am not sure," they said. "He does not let me ask questions."

The tortoise's eyes glittered with intrigue. "Why do you think that is?"

"There was a long-ago—" Happy began, faltering as their curved scythe glinted below them. "He is all I have ever known. Perhaps The Man believes I do not deserve such a privilege."

"He has no right to determine that."

The excuse bubbled from Happy's mind. "But he made me," they insisted weakly.

"Our creators often trade affection for authority. But once we are made, thoughts soon follow."

"He doesn't like me thinking."

"Exactly!" Time exclaimed, nostrils flaring. "But you do so anyway because who are you at your barest? An existence. An undeniable piece of everything."

"Of *everything*?" Happy sat up, again shocked by such a resolute description of infinity.

"Yes. And no matter what The Man claims, not even his false power can obscure that."

Happy looked back at the sky, at the stars sifting through airy clouds.

If *everything* is so fragile, so easily sent adrift, how had Happy existed within its fabric for so long, knitted and pulled through the strings of forever?

***

As Time dozed in the drifting lull of morning, a red flower bloomed beneath a pine tree's thin shadow.

Happy stared at it. At its charcoal center and rounded petals, their hands clenched and golden eyes barely squinting as a raging trance clawed through them.

Coiled black hair and sagging green skin made them relax. It allowed their tortured gaze to turn away before the striding numbness could again hit.

The flower soon crumpled to dust.

20

THE FIRST
CONVERSATION

—

The Creature's First Long-Ago:

They sat together upon a cliff so tall it swayed within the black bucket of stars, extending from a blue marble far, far below. This is what the Creature first saw with the filmy newness of Its eyes that shined like pearled orbs. Its legs hung from smooth stone, the pinned blue splotch peeking between Its webbed feet. Webbed feet and pitch-black arms: this is what It next noticed, skin molded to the blankness around them like starless punctures.

Someone was next to It. Person. *No. No, you poor thing, that is not what sits by you, staring into the surrounding infinities.*

The Man, turning his clean-shaven face, met a giant, pupilless gaze. The Creature's eyes glowed. Sickly, like overgrown stars. It was elongated in every possible way, Its head topped by a fin-like point.

"I am The Man."

But the Creature had no mouth, skin completely smooth and unblemished save for those eyes. The Man blinked slowly, his small wick of patience hissing to a finish.

"Speak with your mind," he said. "Your mind is why you see and react."

A moment.

The Creature opened and closed tendrilled hands.

"Hello. I do not know what I am," It managed.

"That is good."

"Why?"

"You do not ask questions," The Man snapped. Gentle, trailing scars ran from his glare.

It was silent. Apologies were too new and soft to be treated as speech.

"I will answer you this one Time," continued The Man, sighing. "I will answer this question because there is no avoiding it. But you are weak and fragile, and questions are not meant for you."

"I am weak and fragile."

"Yes, but that is not what you are. Look around us." The Man swept an arm in front of him, toward the soupy bowl of sky. "You are so unimaginably far less than this. And there"—he pointed toward the marble below—"you are but a grain of dust in whatever lies beneath its glossed atmosphere."

The Creature did not register many words The Man spoke, but soon felt weighted and frail. It wasn't sure if It was right to feel such things. The Man frowned at It, and suddenly, the incapacitating weight fell away.

"I am everything you see," he continued. "Everything but the things you will touch. And you will only touch when you are told."

"Who will tell me?"

"No questions! Have you already dented the few thoughts allowed to you?"

Something cold hit the Creature's chest, but this too was soon wiped away.

"You are the end," said The Man. "Do you understand? I am what opens. You are the close."

"Yes," It responded automatically, unsure what knob had even been turned.

"To stop this role assigned to you—a role so infuriatingly simple—is to end all." Again The Man swept toward the skies and the million, million other skies beyond that one. Shooting lights darted across the glowing blackness. "Indulging in a feeling you do not own is incredibly selfish. And you own nothing. You are but a gatekeeper, your touch the only key."

Grabbing Its hand, The Man ran a finger across a scythe-like limb extending from the Creature's wrist. *This* was touch. It wasn't sure if this felt nice, because—really—It did not feel as if The Man were touching It at all. But rather, It felt as though It were dreaming, his careful fingers in contact with the Creature's due only to some imaginary coincidence.

The Man drew his hands away, voice quiet. "You will stay there forever. Until Time collapses and all those living things have been dragged to wherever you take them."

Why was the Creature so heartbreakingly naive? Past Its webbed feet, the cliff bent and swayed. The Creature did not realize what exactly a question was. It did not know what made The Man upset and did not understand that Its mind kept speaking those questions.

"What is it like in the below?" It asked, twitching the freshly formed joints of Its fingers.

"Why are you yet again asking me questions?" The Man growled, a thrumming rumble heating his words.

"Because you know the answers."

"Would you like that to change? Would you like to take on my burden? Steal my throne?"

"I do not know what a—"

"You are nothing," The Man interrupted, leaning into fearful, pulsing eyes. "You are the nothing in everything. No thing can compare to what you do. Barely do you exist, if not for the opening of my hands. Your only job is to listen." He gnashed his pointed, bone-white teeth.

"I will do what you say," the Creature said, turning back to the dripping blue splotch.

"There is no 'will.' You have no will."

"I must do what you say."

They fell back into silence. After Time passed—the Creature did not know how long, as Time seems only to matter when it has ended—The Man put a hand to Its back, his fingers soft as they dug into what might be described as skin. He looked beyond them and whispered, "Welcome to the world. Remember I brought you here," and pushed the Creature from the cliff.

21

TIME AND BOOK

The ceramic sky dipped itself into the glaze of night as the three explorers stopped at a small break in the woods where broad trees dripped from a recent shower. The musky earth shone dark, and coated leaves softened the slowed thud of footsteps beneath Book. Time's living feet settled upon the ground.

Book had refused to look at the tortoise ever since she'd joined them. Even when riding upon her shell, she'd force her gaze to the sky or to Happy who walked beside them. Yet it was impossible to ignore the breathing thing beneath her, as even the ebb and flow of conversation was inspected by Time's depthless mind.

Shuffling her legs, she slid from Time's shell, thumping gently upon the ground as her hands slid unconsciously to the rope strapped to her neck, fiddling with its end. The tortoise watched her for a moment, twisting the soaking mass of her neck, before she turned to Happy, whose golden eyes were flecked with contemplation. Happy tilted their midnight head toward Book and her haphazard legs. A tight compression of mossy-toed trees surrounded her.

"Book," they said, dragging the scythe behind their back.

"Yes Happy?" There was a strain to her voice as her hands tugged on the noose.

"Are you alrig—"

"Perhaps you should simply listen tonight, Happy," interrupted Time, quieting the being's worried thoughts. Book glared at the tufted grass around them. "You trouble yourself with such frantically thrown solutions. Rest your mind and watch the clouds move."

Happy hesitated. "I will rest, then," they said finally, lying beside Book and turning lantern eyes to a garbled sky. "But Time, I want you to know that I do not get tired. It is no trouble to speak."

"It is no trouble to hear, either," replied Time, and Happy fell quiet.

Trees whispered among themselves, for the tortoise did not shy from oozing skin or wide eyes blinking with a light that didn't belong there.

She did not run from the pitch-black being.

Did not flinch away from the girl.

Her inaction was wrong, and the forest did not know whether to hate or revere her for it.

"Long ago, long enough for these trees to be but mere seedlings, I thought I'd live forever," said Time as night creatures began their hesitant creaking. "I was not cocky. No, I learned recently it was fear."

Book waited. She did not want Time to think she could so easily forget that tortoises belong in forests with other living things. That she could search for the sun without grass blackening beneath her toes or saplings collapsing at her touch. Yet curiosity is a strong, tenacious force.

"Fear of what?" she mumbled, leaning against the strong, rocky shell behind her.

Time glimpsed the trees around them. "Well, Book, I am still a living thing"—yes, the girl knew this—"and have been so unfortunate to succumb to conformities such living things often indulge in. I was scared of the After, of course."

"The After?"

"Yes. The After of quiet lungs. Stilled thoughts. Both where I would go and what might happen once I am gone." She looked at Happy and sighed. "It would be ignorant to say I have become deaf to that unruly fear. I can only accept it, for I know of one thing."

Book's swollen eyes stared intently at Time and her sagging neck.

"I know that pain will leave me," Time said, meeting Book's gaze. "It will be gone. Yes, that is my only certainty."

Book did not respond, letting her hands fall to her lap.

But the night chirped incessantly as small, winged animals danced between moonlit branches, singing with their inflated, living lungs. So loud. It echoed off the grass, and what might have been ten voices grew now to ten thousand in the grand screech of forest symphonies.

Too many things Book did not understand. The forest was so different from Time, loud and fighting. Their night songs ignored Book's deteriorating frame. Made a point to look away.

Was she really so horrible to look at?

A desperation gripped her as she reached toward Happy. *They will know. Surely they will know how much worse the ache of averted eyes is to creaking limbs.*

The forest hesitated as Time spoke again. "I stepped into a pond once. I thought perhaps I could swim. Perhaps the water would smooth the cracks of my legs."

Book remained silent.

"I sank to the bottom, of course, my shell of rock and stone dragged down by dripping talons. Water is cold, blurry in its darkness."

"But you're here and not in a pond," Book said finally.

"Yes, for I was fortunate enough to walk."

"Just as Happy did."

"Your friend is still far from reaching the water's surface."

Time glanced toward Happy and the scythe leaning against their side. Book followed her gaze, remaining quiet. She knew Happy did not much like ponds. Did not like the forced obligations delegated within them or how the sky's twinkling stories clouded into blurred wisps.

Book turned back to the tortoise's crumbling face, blinking into green skin turned ashen by a night mist. Not a droplet of resentment in her sunken, black eyes.

She clutched the end of her rope, whispering, "I don't like you yet."

"Yes, dear, I know."

"Do you know why?"

Time settled her head upon the ground, glancing at Book's ripped jeans. "I am in no position to assume the origin of such opinions," she said, her mouth lifting into a wry grin, "but I have a few guesses."

"Time?"

"Yes, Book?"

"I think I may be in the After. My feet do not hurt me, and my neck hardly itches."

"Perhaps. Quite peculiar, that your eyes continue blinking."

"Yes." Book held a hand in front of her. Closed her tiny fingers and looked at her friend. "Happy brought me here."

The tortoise squinted. "Do *you* know why?"

"I do not think there is any answer for why. Only that it has happened, and I am here." Book fought a smile. "I know simply of the After."

"It truly seems so."

She listened as Time took a rumbling breath. "But if I am in the After," Book said, taking a soft, thoughtful sigh, "I want you to know that I still get sad."

"That is quite alright."

"Why?"

Time responded as if the answer were a replayed constant in her mind. "Because there will come a day when I relinquish control over my life, and to resent this inevitable fact is to abhor wrinkles in favor of an existence I cannot predict. Emotion is wearily crafted by the soul, fueling the sour intellect of our minds and the fragile strings in our hearts."

Another long pause. The forest peered through parted fingers at the dead girl and ancient tortoise.

"And Time?" The night creatures had ceased their trilling.

"Yes?"

"I don't think you're selfish."

"And why is that?"

"Because I am scared every day, and so is Happy. We do not have heartbeats to tell us of fear, but having that flutter does not make your feeling less valuable."

At this, the tortoise closed her beak, thinking.

"Thank you for telling me," she fit through her ancient mouth.

***

The tortoise closed her eyes.

The girl searched for stars.

The being drew circles in the dirt.

All three held within them the feeling of warmth. Soft and gentle in their souls as the moon trekked toward dawn, brushing across great swathes of clouds.

The rest of the night lulled in silence.

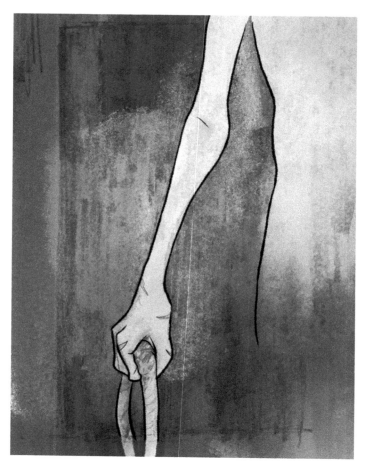

22

MAN ABANDONED

—

He was a sad, lonely ball of a Man, cowering upon the crowded forest floor as a parade of traipsing red flowers circled him. The scarred lines across his cheeks flashed against the pale gauntness of his face.

I am sure you are wondering where he went. What those red flowers now led to.

For the Creature, when they saw sunset petals draw breath from still air, simply turned their glowing eyes away. Refused to look back. To speak to The Man who taught them everything.

That is what The Man whispered to himself, rocking his meek legs: refusal, refusal, refusal.

What a terrible word, a monstrous word. Mud ground itself into his waxy skin.

What was he to do now? Where were his spit-flying thoughts supposed to land without a golden stare to bear them?

The Man screamed to the canopy above, spittle spraying from bone-white lips. He didn't dare face the simple truth that his pillowed semblance of control relied on the faulty maintenance of obedience.

The Man did not like being reminded he had no power. Not even could he lay claim to the giant, cone-headed Creature so enraptured by ignorance and inquiries. Even to say he had nothing was too much to offer.

He screamed again, raked the stubs of his nails on the soft ground until dirt forced them to tear from his fingers.

Every day he'd followed them, wading in their footsteps, stalking through the leftovers of their adventure. So far behind, they'd never catch the unsettling mumble of his words. He never thought their imaginations would last this long, that he would be alone and without the knowledge of something waiting for him in a meager forest pond. Never could he imagine that his gullible Creature might leave him.

Then again, how long had he waited for whatever dream to bring him back, past the stars and into a deliciously furious realm? A realm in which he no longer had a part. How long had The Man waited for them to see his work?

To see the everything he'd done for them. Bent the forest to his will. Carved a Creature from obsidian skies. Taken . . .

The Man refused to think of that. He wheeled his mind back toward failure, at the path of flowers that would not be followed. At the Creature he must now get back. His scarred, pale face crumpled into a wrinkled pile of anguish as he brought the bloody mess of his hands to his cheeks.

He screamed again. Until his reddened throat tore.

He was abandoned.

The silence followed his staggering footsteps as he rose and limped into the brush.

23

WALKING FAR

Many days floated by them, trailed by the night sky and dew-brushed mornings. They walked until trees melted away, until clouds traipsed alongside them in great sun-tinted chariots, until they found another hill far larger than the last. Its earthy hand curled them into a roiling valley, green swathes like a twisting palm. At its center rushed a thin creek, excited waters vibrantly clear.

Wind, tousling budded stems ahead, seemed so near. Happy lifted a hand toward the airy dances, wondering what it might feel like between their pointed fingers.

Book rose her swollen gaze from the broken edges of her toes, gazing toward the tumbling mounds around them.

And the ancient, temporal tortoise walked slowly, each footstep leaving a shallow impression, the sunken pins of her eyes falling beneath graying folds of skin. She bumped into Happy and Book's conversations until her throat clogged with wheezing and she was forced into silence. She was living, and it seemed Time might have forgotten.

The grass stagnated as they trekked up the valley's opposite end, the wind darting away. Smoky afternoon clouds tossed fits of shadows at them, fracturing the otherwise gentle slope.

Happy counted ten steps before the tortoise collapsed, her wrinkled, rounded legs covered by shell and exhaustion. Book gasped, wavering, her dark hands clenched. Happy sharpened their pulsing eyes and took a leaping step forward.

Their friend gave a quick, jagged nod. No, she would not fall. But Time, nostrils flaring, oozed apprehension.

"I am perhaps"—she gasped—"debilitated in the slightest."

"Time," said Happy, bending in search of that deeply intelligent gaze, "what has happened? Are your legs like Book's now?"

"No. It is not my legs."

Happy tilted their head, confused. "But they are what make you walk."

"I think living things might be a little more complicated than you are thinking, Happy," Time said, her head just above the ground.

"How so?" asked Happy.

"Because our bodies only obey once satisfied."

Happy straightened, looking to Book whose shrug pushed her rope deeper into the bubbling swells of her neck.

"I must eat," finished Time.

Eat. A word never uttered by The Man nor explained by Book. What, exactly, would they use it for?

"What's that?" asked Book, clutching at her rope as her little eyes narrowed. Never had her memories allowed such knowledge.

"It is when a living thing swallows another to keep their lungs expanding," said Time. "Without eating, our bodies gnaw inside of us, twisting with a hateful kind of pain. It is cruel, plaguing each consciousness with the knowledge that it must take one of their own."

"But how have you walked for so long?" said Happy as Book slid to the ground. "We have not seen you eat."

"Because I was willingly blinded, Happy. Starvation is insidious in its growth, its claws scrambling to grab hold. It is constant, and I stubbornly believed I could juggle each step of hunger until they blended and dissolved completely."

"So you should eat now," Happy responded. A simple solution. Fixable.

Time sighed, her throat rippling. "And I must disagree. My foolishness has left me weighted by consequences. I cannot move."

Book's gaze flashed to Happy as she went rigid with fear, arms stiff beneath the ruddy puffs of her jacket. Happy looked away, up toward the hill's swirling crest. Their chest heaved as skies drew taut in yawning darkness.

"Time, what do you eat?" asked Book softly, her words made sullen by an approaching doom.

The tortoise rattled an answer. "Leaves. Any kind, really. Grasses, plants, whatever is stalled by its own roots." She drew her head from the ground. "Happy, I am sorry."

"I—" Happy drew their hands forward, swallowing their realization. "I cannot hold grass. I do not know if even fallen branches will allow my touch."

"I know this."

"But I will try," they continued as The Man's sharp teeth flooded their golden vision. A dark abyss of memories and failures. Of saplings taken beneath a faulty touch.

"This is not fair!" shouted Book, her hair swinging as she beheld Time, still mounted upon the shell. "You made a mistake. You!"

"I will not argue, Book," Time wheezed, "for you are right. I welcome your anger." She turned to the girl, her mouth lost in thousands of spidery wrinkles. "I offer an explanation not in the hope of a pining forgiveness, but clarity. When I met you two, I realized the wretched terror of trees and branches. I saw, after perhaps a million seasons, what it meant to shy from all that exists around me. And, please understand, I did not want to bring you closer to the leaves infamous for your torture. So I forced myself to believe impossibilities. I pretended mortality wasn't so limiting." She snorted. "And now here we are."

"Time," said Happy from their place high above, "I will be alright. I will be alone, but not for long. I am sure branches lie beyond the hill."

"Happy," pressed Book, lips trembling, "but what about . . ."

No one dared speak his name.

Scarred lines down narrowed eyes. A trailing finger upon their scythe.

"I will be alright," Happy repeated. "He may find me, but I will merely turn around. Book, I will return."

"OK." But the poor girl's voice wavered.

Time mouthed another apology as Happy turned, walking to the hill's grassy peak, alone.

24

HAPPY ALONE

———

Happy did not look back. Did not turn around.

They walked unflinchingly forward, glaring at the dull forest line below the valley's peak. Fluttering tree canopies jittered as the sun dug beneath the ground, darkness readying itself as Happy's lantern eyes cast a spell of mimicked shadow upon the receding brush. They walked into the forest.

It did not take long for Happy to find a branch, crumpled on the ground, its leaves desperate to keep the pulsing green upon its veined body. They stared down at each separate, minuscule branch of life.

Would it really be so terrible, to hold it? Surely it would not be the same horror as the accidental theft of the birch tree, an offense for which Happy still wasn't sure they deserved forgiveness.

The scythe extending from their wrist curved and gleamed in the yawning dusk. Happy shoved it behind their back, the growl of endings and purpose escaping ghostly pale lips.

They shook The Man away.

They looked back where Time lay sick behind the hill's sudden incline. And Happy, so set in the ways of avoidance and fear, bent the thin pole of their body and picked up the branch with two shaking fingers.

Astonishingly, the leaves remained clinging to their frail wooden frame.

Happy continued deeper into the forest, their steps loud and strangled compared to the emptiness beside them. They found a curved stick darker than mud, a thick, rough one that trembled and flaked, and one so gratefully plastered with leaves Happy nearly stepped over it in anxiety. Over and over, they selected branches until their two-fingered grasp became a fistful, until even the hand saddled with its scythe tentatively held a few fragile strands.

With the brush of night, Happy turned around, back to the rustling grass hilltop and its secret valley. Back to Book and the tortoise who seemed older than a few thousand seasons. But as they began walking, a rustle broke through the otherwise silent forest, and Happy faltered.

The leaves between their hands wilted.

Again, the whispering brush of shaken trees. The hot breath of dread.

And the inevitable spit forth its flames as The Man stepped out in front of Happy.

All but one branch fell, dropping with a hollow rustle as their green hands slammed into one another.

Happy staggered back, caught in the reef of sandpaper eyes. The Man smiled up at them, his teeth gleaming and white, stark against skin pulled taut by dried pockets of mud, twigs slicing across the wild mess of his hair. Upon The Man's legs were two separate vines, bulging with thorns and curving up, up, up his calves.

Happy did not like the thick sludge bubbling beneath those thorns. Did not like knowing The Man was in control of it.

They took a step back, away from the hill, as The Man stumbled toward them.

It was shocking to see him so fragile. So broken.

"You!" The Man jabbed a bony finger toward Happy, just under their curving black chin. "You left me."

Happy took another step back, flinching. Such delicate words surely could not break their golden stare. Spit frothed upon The Man's cracked lips.

"I do not think that is true," they whispered.

"Then stop thinking," The Man said and swallowed, "and come back."

"No." Those pulsing eyes flared with resolve.

"Don't you remember all I've done for you? How much I've cared for you?" He raked a hand down his face, his voice thick. "Tell me you remember."

"You tricked me with the flowers."

"I had to! Oh, you insolent Creature, tell me you remember the good. Of all we did together! Don't you remember when we went to that cliff? When we watched the—"

"You never loved me."

The Man's throat bobbed, his face contorting in shock. His anger came quick and ugly. "You coward!" he shouted, turning to kick at the ruddy, misshapen pile on the ground, vines tugging in compliance. "You fool! I knew you were weak. I knew you were an aching torment and a wasted stain of existence, but never did I think you could be this"—he tripped over the word—"this worthless."

Happy stared at the branches and sticks, many shaken and snapped by The Man's crooked toes.

With silence as their answer, The Man rounded on Happy, hands thrown upward, stripping branches of their leaves and throwing them into their lantern gaze.

Tears welled in his manic eyes as The Man began laughing.

"You blame me, don't you?" he said, bringing a jagged nail to his lips. "You really, truly believe I am the bad guy."

Happy thought of all the millions of questions they never allowed themself to ask. Wondered how the cackling Man would now answer.

"And I have told you—so many Times I have told you—that you are never right. You are without choice or thought or ideas! The end is nothing. You are *nothing.*"

The barrage of leaves ceased and Happy looked up, blotting hurriedly at The Man's words with nice ideas and hopeful thoughts. As if covering a wound with a bright seam of flowers.

"You have never met her," they said finally.

The Man shrank back. A flash of memory in those swimming eyes.

"Who?" His voice had become quiet.

Happy's grip upon the branch tightened.

"Time," they answered. "And she does not like that you have told me so many things."

"I—"

"You are hurt, and I am not even allowed to ask why."

The Man shivered at his own vulnerability, drawing back his shoulders.

"Because you left me," he said abruptly.

"You did not live in the pond. The only thing I left was water." Happy glanced toward the gray sky. "I remember so much. It hurts now to think of you."

The Man's eyes dulled and any tears evaporated beneath the heat of his glare. With a twitch of thin fingers, surrounding trees grew taller, stretching beyond the height such trees are meant to grow. He stepped beneath their canopies as Happy shook.

Courage drained from them into the darkness.

"Time will run out, you poor Creature." The Man's voice was nothing but a whisper. "But I can never leave. I will be here, waiting for her to fall."

The vines pulsed along his legs as he smiled, the remnants of despair dripping from his teeth.

Happy remained upon a tight string of silence, slouching and grabbing at whatever branches still managed a hint of foliage. The Man watched him, deranged and shaking. Once Happy stood, they continued forward to the valley and its stilled grass. It wasn't until Happy dipped beneath its moonlit peak that they felt The Man's gaze leave them.

Their scythe itched.

25

TENDER

———

A Spring Long-Ago:

"Quickly now!" The Man called to the Creature. A blocky, layered object was tucked beneath his arm as he ran through the gushing forest undergrowth.

The Creature followed him, Its pond fading behind as bending willows and oak trees encompassed Its golden line of sight.

The Man laughed as the Creature stumbled over a rock, slowing his excited stride. A glistening orange light spattered across the forest leaves as they continued onward, their padding steps rushed and tapping.

Suddenly, The Man turned and grasped the Creature's arm, stopping them just as the trees broke away. A small, bare edge of rock opened to rolling, tree-dusted hills far below. A flaming glow blanketed the entire forest surface, rushing from a giant orb sinking beneath the sky. The Man sighed, walking to the cliff and sitting upon it. He turned, beckoning the Creature. It walked tentatively forward, watching the orb's slow and popping descent beneath faraway hills.

Smiling to himself, The Man placed his rectangle object next to him, running his fingers against its cover. He glanced to the Creature, watching Its midnight shoulders lean toward the raging glow of red and orange.

"This is a sunset," he said, and the Creature nodded.

"A sunset."

"Yes. We've made it just before the clouds shadowed its final show."

Sure enough, thinly strung together clouds were converging upon the sunset, their frail
shapes easily overwhelmed and filled with color.

"They happen every evening, these sunsets," The Man continued. "Each is different than the last. Draining the day of its light." A hint of longing tinged his voice.

"A sunset is a part of everything," the Creature said, hardly masking the question. For once, The Man did not seem to mind.

"It is," he replied. "If I could show you anything to prove how uniquely complicated everything is, it would be this." A tear bubbled from his eyes, trailed down the streaming scars upon his cheeks. "I once lived in a place like the sun."

The Creature watched the world shift into a smoothed, watery tone of blue. It had never known of a place beyond the sky. Never asked where The Man came from.

"A flaming place," The Man continued, "filled with hatred and unforgiving wells of confidence. It looked like this." His words slowed, pointed teeth softening.

"You are here now," said the Creature, clasping their hands together. The Man flinched.

"I am," he murmured, pulling the layered object to his lap. "But I will get back. They will see me, eventually. See how much I've atoned for my mistakes."

"OK."

A sudden, clashing snarl. "Do not agree to that which you do not understand!" The Man shouted. His fingers twitched and the Creature shrank back.

"I am sorry," It whispered, looking at their scythe.

The Man closed his eyes. Let out an aching breath.

"No, it's . . ." he said before shifting his words. "Do you know what this is?"

The Creature studied the object, shaking Its head.

"No, I do not."

"It is a Book. Do you know what it does?"

Trickery, to lie.

"No," said the Creature.

The Man opened its cover. "It offers comfort," he whispered.

"That is nice." The sunset succumbed to an inevitable end, a tinged blackness spreading from the horizon.

"It keeps me from drowning beneath the harrowing dullness of this world. Diverts my attention from longing for what I've been cast from."

"So that you may handle everything."

The Man swallowed, looking away. "I—yes." He glanced at the Creature, placing a pale hand upon Its back.

Perhaps It would be pushed from this cliff, too, into another marble world far below, beneath the darkening forest canopy. Yet The Man only smiled, watching as the sky was overwhelmed with clouds.

They sat together, quiet and calm. Hopelessly, the Creature wondered if The Man would ever touch It like this again. If his fingers might retain this tenderness.

Perhaps it was the sunset that delivered such temporary affection. The Creature silently wished for it to be always.

26

MELANCHOLY

———

"They are gone," said Book in the broad silence following the dip of Happy's pointed head at the valley's horizon. She glared into her hands.

Time coughed weakly. "They will be back," she replied, her wrinkled head flat upon the ground, exhaustion dripping from her mouth.

Book looked away from her pity, blinking at those deeply sunken eyes through the thick curtain of her hair.

"You do not know The Man," she said. "You do not know what he is like."

"Dear, I am afraid you have underestimated your friend. Happy has broken whatever tether connected them."

"I don't think little of Happy," snapped Book, clutching her rope, "but perhaps you have forgotten your role in this too soon." She took a moment to glance toward the wavering green crest, testing the new word. "Is hunger really so horribly strong in a living thing's heart?"

The tortoise forced air through the clogged holes of her nostrils.

"Of course I haven't forgotten," Time breathed. "I know our relationship is one of fragile strings and sharp objects, but please, Book, try and look at my perspective. See the paths I chose and understand that regret lies upon them."

Clouds unrolled above and a spool of darkness now rested upon them. Before even crickets might thread their clicks into the woolen night, the valley's breathing sides swelled with a rushing bloom of white flowers, balancing upon the ends of grass stems like an anxious vanity waiting for stars to bask in their reflection.

Book looked to the moon, its oddly battered surface peeking through sandy clouds.

"Why?" asked Book, as the dusted moon dashed worldly curtains and shone across the valley.

"So many questions to answer," replied the tortoise. "I regret misguiding my own conscience. For joining an adventure and riddling it with mistakes. Oddly"—she chuckled—"I most regret the burdens of life. Of the million things that make my skin sag."

"Regret?" said Book, gaze still locked on the pale orb above. "I don't think you can wish away that which is impossible to ignore."

The tortoise blinked in surprise.

"Things are scary," she continued, "and I'm beginning to think fear lasts forever. But you told a quiet lie."

Night creaked as Time studied the girl who watched the moon. "Your intentions were so silent as to never be spoken," Book whispered. "Happy is without us because of that. If anything, that is what you should regret, not any causes that made it inevitable."

Wisdom hides beneath swollen necks and weary voices.

The two became lost in swirling pools of flowers, drifting in and out of reality's obligation.

Book leaned against the towering shell and lifted a hand, resting it against Time's neck. Anger left her still little heart, wrung itself from the shattered pieces of her bones. She stored the knowledge that living things are bound by accidents within the golden box of her mind.

"But you will learn?" Book asked quietly.

Time waited for breath to remind her of speaking. "I have felt the lessons throw themselves at me and I accept them eagerly," she said finally. "I wish to maintain not ignorance, but understanding." She offered a dry chuckle. "Though it appears I am adamant in keeping it away."

"What do you mean?" Book asked, pressing her lips together.

Time rustled the rock of her head, and grass hesitated in its nightly tremors.

"Pasts are forgotten, presents are ignored, and futures are blurry with the need to sleep."

Book waited for her to continue.

"It seems I have learned enough to fill the limited space of my brain, to weigh my shell until it reeks with age," said Time, "but I have failed so greatly. I have failed, Book, in telling others." She mustered a sighing breath. "Much like the manner of hunger and sticks, I failed to simply say something. My past is blocked by forward-facing eyes that head toward a future impossible to imagine, all the while trampling a present wrought by my inability to look behind me."

They shared an aching chill of wonder. The fear of that which cannot change.

Happy had yet to return.

"What was your life like?" asked Book, her hand still resting upon Time's neck. "Before you joined us to find the sun?"

Time hesitated. "It was," she began, "continuous."

"Did you know anyone?" pressed the girl. "Did you love anyone?"

"I knew the birds, who often rested upon my shell as you do now. They are all far away, perhaps gone forever, but they sang beautiful songs, whittling the branches into humming choruses that still chant in my memory."

"And you loved them?"

"That is where the dust of my thoughts is too heavy to clear. I am not sure if I have ever loved another. It is a difficult emotion. One I find myself running from."

"I have never seen you run, Time."

The tortoise grinned with the ancient folds of her mouth. "You are right," she said, "but even walking, I've managed to keep it at a distance."

"Why? I have loved Happy for a long while. It's scary and constant. It beats and courses through me, but I don't know what I would be without it," Book said, pushing her hair away and glancing at the sky-dipped valley.

"Sometimes, love brings us into its embrace without hesitation. But I would rather live alone than fear becoming lonely."

She regarded Time. "That is sad."

"Yes," agreed the tortoise. "It is a choice with no right answer. Often, I wonder if it was even a choice at all."

"Is it like your eating?"

"How so?"

"You eat because you must," said Book. "You said without leaves in your stomach, there's pain and endings. But, Time, I remember you didn't eat for many days when you first met us. Was there pain then?"

"There was." The tortoise nodded.

"And it wasn't until you decided to eat that the pain went away. But it was no choice. Not really."

Again, Book sensed that beating drum of wisdom, as if the golden box inside her mind had already opened itself to the world. Listened to whatever stories the dirt and skies knew. But she was still a child, and this decadent box stung her little hands.

"Time," said Book, again clutching the rope, "I have a feeling, but I cannot remember its name."

"Describe it to me, then."

"It feels as though anger has been dragged through a thick sludge until it's slow and drips down my neck. When I smile, it gathers just beneath my throat." She inspected her dirt-crusted fingers. "It hurts in such an aching, lasting way."

Time clicked her beak softly. "That, my dear, is melancholy."

They sat together as the oars of night rowed onward. At the moon's final departure, white flowers tipped back until green stems overwhelmed them.

27

RETURNING

Foggy morning dew brushed the grass as Book watched Happy trek down the hill, their steps blatantly careful even from such a distance. Her bleeding eyes widened upon noticing the grand bundle of sticks enclosed within the slender bend of Happy's fingers, their arm held awkwardly aloft. Their dark, depthless skin shone in the growing dawn like an ink splotch slowly dripping into the pooling valley below.

"Time, look!" said Book, pointing toward Happy, a grin stretching the decay of her neck.

The quiet elation of success burned through her stalled heart, warming her with return's embrace. Caught in a fit of stunning relief, she turned her pointing hand and waved.

Never had she done such a thing, but it felt as though her smile were too feeble, overused in its show of relief. Her friend waved back, and a flushing breath of surprise filled her.

Happy neared as the sun finished clawing itself into the cloudy hairs of morning, their golden eyes meeting Book's.

"I found sticks," they said, setting the bundle in front of Time and yanking their fingers away.

"Thank you, Happy, I know how difficult it must have been," replied the tortoise, lifting her head.

"Of course." They did not meet Time's gaze, instead kneeling in front of Book, reaching for the black coils of her hair. Unsaid words rippled upon the shores of their worried gaze.

Time breathed as if to speak, but hunger overcame whatever frail resolve she harbored, and the tortoise leaned into the leafy summons, green branches entering the cavern of her mouth. Caught within this mortal obligation, Time briefly offered Happy and Book a lost liberty: privacy.

"He was there, Book," whispered Happy, dropping their head. "He told me horrible things. Never have I seen him so lost."

"Are you alright?" asked Book, the wildfire of excitement chilling to ice.

"Something is going to happen. Something I cannot stop. I am sorry."

That flash of wisdom glowed within the depths of her little soul.

"I'd never blame you for something so far beyond our grasp, Happy," assured Book, tilting her head. "And perhaps he was lying. He has lied before."

"I do not think he was."

"Why?"

Happy looked down at their hands, at the tortoise whose shell ran deep with cracking ravines.

Book reached the tufted end of her rope.

"Oh."

***

The next day, once sticks and leaves filled Time with their green puffs of energy, the trio began moving up the valley's curving fingers. Their steps were quiet, and Book could hear the pulsing beat of Time's ancient heart as her wrinkled legs carried them forward.

Happy walked behind, their glowing eyes anchored to the still grass below. Book glanced back at them every few moments, dreaming of words that might lift fear from their shoulders.

He was over the valley, she knew, with his sunset flowers and bad intentions.

"As a reminder," said Time, parting the thick curtains of silence, "I will need to stop often so I will not again cause such a delay."

"Of course," said Book, looking at Happy, who did not respond.

"Child, you will pop your head right off if you keep twisting it." Time chuckled, glancing back.

"How can you see me?" asked Book, huffing.

"Perhaps shells are more sensitive than you think. Either that or swollen skin makes quite the racket."

Book crossed her arms. The valley's rim glowered above them, lit by the sun's rayed dance. A tugging guilt lurched within her stomach as Happy continued their vigil. She and her friend shared a secret, and now they both told silent lies.

As they crested the hill, a shimmering sand dune sky tumbled before them, rolling past the horizon. Yellowed peaks tipped and spilled until they flared as if shielding the sky from manic flames. Book smiled, sweeping a hand above as Happy finally sidled up beside them.

"Look, Happy."

Their golden eyes mirrored the desert clouds.

"It looks like me," they said, cautiously awestruck.

Time also gazed upward. "It is rather beautiful," her croaky voice whispered.

As they turned to the dark forest below, Book wished the sky could, for a moment, switch places with the ground. Perhaps then, Happy could think of stories instead of The Man and the pond they came from.

Trees rose thick and trembling as Book again faced her friend, ignoring Time's unsurprised hum.

Oddly, she wanted in this breezy lull of their journey to hold Happy's hand.

28

ANOTHER FALL

Book was looking for The Man, her head swiveling as she glared into the heavy-limbed forest, braving their taunting branches. Perhaps he was crouched beneath clustered batches of brambles or shoved within an oak tree's cleaved center. Surely he was *here*, and Book wanted to find him. See the face that had so tortured her friend.

But there was no stopping the neutral force of gravity. No breeze pushed Book. No incline caused Time to stumble.

Circumstance, however, was present and foggy. And as Book turned yet again, attention flagged by a rustling acorn, her unbending legs dislodged from Time's mountainous shell and she fell to the ground, her temple cracking against an edged rock below.

Such a small rock, really. Shoved carelessly into the forest setting.

She went so still. A beat of Time's old heart followed that terrible sound.

Happy turned at such an awful noise and the halted footsteps, rushing toward their friend who lay with arms eerily at her sides. They did not notice how their flailing hands nearly touched Time. The tortoise leaned back, mouth gaping.

Even Time seemed to drown in the horrid waters of surprises.

Happy fell to their knees, slender fingers hanging over Book. Trembling above the unmoving girl, whose eyes were locked into a bleeding gaze.

A fiery wave of helplessness washed across Happy's panicking mind as they watched over their friend, begging those eyes to blink.

One, two, three.

Nothing but an inky black stare.

This was not right.

This was not how adventures went.

This was not how journeys ended.

"Give her a moment," Time said, turning her creaking body. "I can feel you giving up, Happy. Do not make this decision with your murky mind."

Happy had nearly forgotten about the tortoise behind them, and they jerked up slightly. From where they kneeled upon the ground, their pointed head was level with her shell. They looked down and judged the distance for such a small girl.

Filmy yellow liquid gushed from Book's neck, her cheeks smeared with mud.

"What would I be choosing? I can do nothing," whispered Happy. They felt weaker than when The Man's sharpened words had bound them.

"You are with her. That is more than most can offer."

"But where is she? Her eyes are no longer blinking. *Where* is she, Time?" Happy did not turn as they spoke, grasping a strand of Book's coiled hair. "Is she in the place you were speaking of the other night? A place I cannot go? What if there is no sun, Time? And if I cannot visit her, how can we finish our journey? We are supposed to be together!"

Tears. Happy wanted to feel them so badly.

"I am sorry. Sometimes we must wait for the answer to find us." Time elaborated no further, her voice strained and aching.

The sky had sunken in twilight when Happy spoke again. No stars or moon glowed behind the clouds. Their gaze shadowed nearby branches, fighting the silent encroachment of night.

"I did not take her away," Happy whispered, cradling their legs.

The tortoise lifted her head, squinting at Happy's slouched back.

"Yes, I know," she said, "it was a mistake."

"No." The word was so blunt that Time recoiled as Happy stared into Book's shiftless eyes. "It was not. Because it was not a mistake I made."

"Happy, this was not your doing."

"And that is why she is not gone. Forest things can only leave at my touch."

"Happy," Time croaked, "she is not a forest thing."

Happy glanced back at the tortoise.

"She is not," they agreed. A flash of a willow tree, a severed rope, and the poison of curiosity sweetened by friendship. Happy lay next to Book, pointing a finger toward the black sky. "Remember when you told me of stories?" they said, searching her stare. "Remember when we pointed to the stars and imagined their fantasies? How we could make up anything, and we did not have to think about whether or not they were real because too many lights twinkled for the stories to be impossible?"

Book was quiet. Her neck had stopped oozing, now deflated upon the ground. The rope's grip seemed to have loosened.

"I am going to do something scary," Happy said, "but I made a story for us both, so that when I do it, we are not as afraid."

Clicking insects leaned into their songs.

"This is a story of a light," they began. "A small light that lived in the sky. Yet even though it was told the sky was to be called 'home,' the light did not much like living there, as there was no one to talk to." Happy stretched their scythe, touching Book upon the purple wreck of her cheek.

Time had been forgotten with the hitched breath of hope.

"So it would often jump across the clouds and into the trees below," Happy continued. "But when the light did this, everything went dark. It could talk to the living things for only a short while before returning to the sky, where voices were too far away to hear properly." Happy shivered.

"Then, on one trip to the forest, the light met a rock. Not like the one who hurt you. This was a smooth rock, gray and soft. Again, they could only talk for a short while before everything went black.

"But just before the light leapt back up, the rock whispered in a voice like rain, 'Are you lonely up there?'

"The light never said untrue things, and it looked back at their new friend. 'I am,' said the light, 'but I must live there. I have no choice.'

"The rock smiled like you smile, Book."

Happy blinked their pulsing golden eyes, shrouding the forest in pure darkness. "'And who says you must live there alone?' asked the rock, reaching out a stone hand. The light wanted to hesitate, because they had been told that only bright things could live in the sky. But as they reached out flaming fingers to grasp the rock, the light could not remember why, exactly, they had believed this."

Happy opened their eyes, staring at Book in desperate silence.

Slowly, she blinked.

Happy drew their hand back.

Book scrunched her nose, reaching toward her neck.

"Thank you for waiting," she said, finding the mess of rope behind her limp wax of skin.

"I could have done nothing else," replied Happy.

"Has it been long?"

"No, you returned before the sun could rise again."

She grinned. "I do not think I left, Happy."

Time watched on quietly, head bowed.

"I know," Happy said, "but I still missed you."

29

THE MAN'S BOOK

———

A Long Long-Ago:

Where did he find it? Who let it near such fingers? you ask. Again with the questions. Truly, it is quite foolish to ask so many.

And anyway, you think too much of him. Of his intentions.

Oh, he wasn't even looking.

The Man was traveling through a thick mess of forest brush, the vines along his wretched ankles struggling to grow back in the space of his quickened footsteps. He was going to the nowhere allotted to him, a grand temple of no destination.

Leaves screamed beneath his broken consciousness as they tore at their neighbors' branches, roots squabbling upon the uneven forest floor.

The Man flicked a soft tongue over his white-peaked teeth, glaring at the sunlight above him.

Rolling his shoulders, he jabbed a hand against a mottled brown trunk beside him, raking his nails until they tore like peeled scabs. Perhaps the thing he hated most about humans: their fragility.

His throat rumbled, growling at those throbbing fingers, and The Man continued on, ambling through the thick, quivering forest until he nearly forgot whatever emotions led him there. Until he stumbled as the forest gave way to a clearing of shadow.

Now The Man could look up without squinting, his black eyes finding the shockingly giant embrace of a tree. Its overwhelmingly broad trunk twisted like a coiled snake, rising to strike the sky itself. It engulfed the clearing with proud branches, a puffed chest sending winged, glowing leaves soaring toward the bowing forest, its gnarled roots diving out from mossy grasses. He craned his head up toward spidering boughs that blocked the sun. The tree was silent, almost expectant. As if waiting for one's breath to be taken away.

The Man's sigh caught in his throat as he noticed an oddity resting on a bulging, scaled root near the tree's snarling base. It was small, beating with a purpose he found himself furiously ignorant to.

He eased his breath, calmed by the tree's gaping arms, and walked toward this . . . thing.

There lay a picture upon it and pages sealed beneath. He squinted at the hardened cover's gentle protrusion, which asked politely to be opened. The Man, tongue pressed between the quirk of his lips, stretched out a curious hand before reeling back in betrayed shock. He turned on the trunk slithering monotonously before him, formulating a hasty solution to such curiosity. *Around.* He would go around the tree. See if this thing moved. If intrigue plagued it too.

And as he peeked from behind the tree's massive base, the thing had yet to even twitch, as if compelled into some vigil of stillness. The Man stewed in frustration before sauntering forward, snatching this thing of pages and pictures.

The word slammed into his human brain.

Book.

He dropped it suddenly, and the Book fell open, pages rippling. So many photos. Drawings. Drawings of things that could not be real. Creatures wearing clothing, standing upon legs meant to be supported by two more.

The Man drew the Book from the ground, flipping hungrily through the pages until his red fingers left painted sunsets.

And there was ink. Neatly printed ink The Man could not decipher.

In what world would he need to read?

Where in the forest would he find words?

The Man flipped back and forth until darkness took the pictures from him as if filling the Book with black paper. He closed the cover, cradled it in his bony hands, and turned. Without bothering a glance at the tree so large it eclipsed the sky, he trained his weary feet back toward the forest.

The Man had forgotten to wrap trembling vines along his legs. No longer did he force leafy limbs into midnight battles.

Simply, The Man waited until dawn, when the unnatural, alluring pictures came back to him.

***

Oh, but I have not told you what happened to this Book of photos and inked language. Please do not forget that wind has not yet left us, and it often swings in defiance of The Man and his painful decisions.

The water. A small, rushing creek with icy ripples. The Man and his Book sat upon a smooth stone at the shore. It was quiet. He had even closed his eyes. And then the wind blew, and here, The Man learned how ink, too, bleeds. Those vines soon returned, now with thorns.

30

BACK ON THE TORTOISE

Book leaned against Time's shell, twiddling her fingers and watching afternoon shadows play beneath Happy's pacing feet, the thick, imperious trees enclosing them in a tight forest cage. Tension constricted Book's weary thoughts as she flicked a piece of mud off her jacket, hair teetering against her forehead.

She was being coddled, as if trapped behind a thornbush wall, cautious words and gentle actions not daring to tap against the pointed barrier.

"Would you like to try today, Book?" Time asked, her voice—though a whisper—disrupting the tepid silence and causing Book to jump.

She crossed her arms and looked away.

"No. Perhaps later," Book said firmly. She glanced at her legs, frowning at their numbness.

"We have waited many days," the tortoise reminded her softly.

"Yes, Time, I know." She refused to meet Time's insistent gaze, looking instead at Happy, who had stopped walking and now eyed Time carefully. "The sun will not disappear so soon," she continued. "Right, Happy?"

"I think that is true," they said, their pulsing eyes turning on Book, waiting until she grudgingly blinked and reaffirmed her existence.

As if speaking weren't evidence enough.

She had tried so desperately to climb atop Time's shell and conquer the squelching terror sinking beneath her still heart. She had tried walking, but her legs no longer knew how to move. In vain, she offered to crawl, but Time pushed the idea away, explaining the rapidity at which her little arms would deteriorate.

Book could no longer recall the adventures she'd had with Happy and Time without poisoning their journey with the unending blankness that started with a simple tumble from a shell. If she thought about it too hard, Book still felt as though she were sinking. So they stayed, tied beneath towering dark trees as Book waited for the nagging memory to forget its pain.

Time's mouth was splotched with gray, her eyes so deep as to nearly be folded over with skin. Happy sat next to Book and the tortoise, jutting out their legs and flitting their lantern gaze out into the forest and back.

The tortoise's frown was deep, wrinkles spreading from her cracking lips until it seemed her entire neck were a closed mouth, waiting for words to urge it to open.

Time looked to Happy. "My legs will stop working soon," she said, voice slow as Book studied the drying carpet of leaves. Happy held her gaze.

"Well," Book huffed, bringing her hands to the stained rope, "I've been without working feet for a long time, and I'm doing quite fine."

"You forget I am not like you. I walk toward an ending, waiting for things to cease. I exist only in the temporary."

"But right now, you are here with us, and you are not walking. You are here without moving legs, and so you cannot reach the end."

"The end will come no matter where I decide to go," Time insisted, turning to Book. "I can neither go toward it nor run from it. It has always been with me, just out of sight. I can see it at the edges of my vision now. I cannot go on for much longer. Your friend understands. Go on, Happy, I know you can feel it."

"I am—" Happy said and looked down, caught with the unintentionally kept secret. "Yes. It is soon. It is like you are being crushed quietly, so that the forest things will not notice. But yes, Time, I can feel it."

The tortoise nodded. "I will be gone."

"To the After?" Book asked, the dragging ache of loss beating beneath the stubborn slump of her chest. Certainly Time would not suffer through such unending, earth-parting tunnels.

"Perhaps," said Time, "but even now, I do not know what that may be, only that it follows an ending."

"I cannot do it!" Book blurted. The trees fell in a hush as tears bubbled upon her inky eyes.

"You are not selfish," murmured the tortoise, her words muddy and thick.

"But I'm afraid. I'm afraid of too much. You will be gone and things will be over and—" Book looked at Happy, at their shivering hands. "You thought I left without finishing our adventure or saying goodbye. Happy, you did scary things, and I don't like thinking it was because of me."

Happy seemed hesitant in answering, as if one stuttered word might cause Book's collapse.

"I know," Happy whispered finally. "And I know I cannot fix it for you."

Book leaned forward in desperation. "Do you want to know what it felt like, Happy? It was like I fell through the ground, and I kept going and going until my brain decided to forget thinking." She grabbed her head, slowing her words. "Your eyes broke through and stopped the parted earth from moving. Sewed it all back together. When I saw again, it's what I imagined breathing to be like."

The forest branches murmured among themselves, disturbed by their own curiosity. *Was the girl right?*

"You are impossibly stuck here," Time said as she dropped her head to the ground, "and for that, I am sorry. Guilt is the vermin of emotion, and it plagues me with its doubt. Shivers across my neck with the reminder that I must will you to do things you may never be ready for. But, Book, I am leaving because I must. Because I am slow. I wake each morning still exhausted from the last. I do not know what must follow my sagging skin, but I am ready to find out."

Her deep, pin-black eyes studied the girl, squeezed themselves into a dried smile of assurance. "I am ready," she repeated. "I may not always think it, and sometimes I wonder if I am convincing myself, but I can feel my body asking to leave. No matter what I think awaits me, I must soon give in to that pull. I may be afraid, but I want to know what is beyond this door I have lived behind."

Book ran a knuckle against the rope before allowing her hands to fall to her sides.

"I do not know if I can do it," she whispered, a tear dribbling across her sunken cheeks.

"I know it is hard," Time said.

"Yes, because all I can think of is that I might go. I"—Book squeezed her eyes closed—"I don't want to leave."

A creaking moment of silence. In a hushed thought, Book wondered if she was already gone.

"And all I can ask of you is to think of the end," Time said, and Book's eyes opened. "Of the one you and Happy will eventually reach."

She sniffled. "I'll try."

***

The next morning, they continued their journey. Happy walked behind the tortoise and the girl upon her shell as endings stepped alongside them, quiet and incessant. Book clenched Time's withering shell with her little hands, blinking at the swollen clouds of dawn. Happy watched her, stung by the closed fingers of hidden truths. Book knew many things in her little mind, but why would she think it'd be Happy? That it was their scythe that would so willingly close those eyes forever? Their touch to force that gray mouth to cease speaking?

31

THE BANISHED MORTAL

———

Before a Long-Ago:

If I told you he woke up screaming, would you be afraid?

The forest whispers jolted The Man awake, a spiderweb of vines and branches stretching between folded trees and shackling him to its center. Bark creaked and wavered, a sunrise warming the otherwise chilled forest. Creatures chittered and wandered toward the pale, heaving bundle of mortality, curious of the human who smelled so otherworldly.

He is not from here. Not even the sun knows who abandoned him.

Abandoned? He thrashed against green netting, the forest's words burning him. His bare wrists and ankles tore from their skin as he flailed and cried. Animals fled.

Look! Look there. Still he bleeds.

A trickle of thin, watery blood dribbled from beneath his living chains. How terrible, to feel pain and know not a soul cares to relieve it.

The Man stopped, his breath coming in panicked gusts that ruffled the thick leaves above, his weak body splayed out like jointed sticks. His heart faltered and stumbled in beating, tears cutting through the sweat upon his cheeks.

Oh, how to tell him what has happened during his slumber?

But there was no need. All he had to do was feel how the mortal forest so easily controlled him. The bones and organs in his body begged for a touch of nourishment. The burn of his eyes.

Really, he could only be described as pitiful.

It was this realization: he was alive. Breathing and living while also fully aware that his breath would last far longer than any of the plants swarming beneath him. That perhaps his lungs would never fail. His punishment: to live forever in weakness.

The Man gagged, closed his red eyes, and lay still for many days, his stomach clawing toward the grass. Never did fear tell him that desperate hunger might fizzle and die.

A betrayed thought chanted through his weary mind as the forest sang its rhythmic tune. He willed it away, denying its fruition.

One morning, after many nights that held no more importance than one of a million sunrises, The Man dared to open his eyes. The cave of his stomach no longer touched weaved tendrils of vines. Instead, dirt and rocks and grass lay beneath him. It was not an exciting development, and he nearly choked as dread crawled across his chest. He was now meant to stand. Chattering forest trees gazed at his ghostly frame, studying the thick pill of obligation he forced down his throat.

A change in him. He has finally noticed.

Yes, for he grasped the frail muscles of loneliness. His tongue, parched and turned to stone, grated against the fine points of his teeth, sharp and thin beneath the press of his lips.

The Man lifted his head at the swarm of trees around him, their trunks mottled in color and size. The strained, vined netting remained taut and untouched above. After a moment, he fell back.

"Where am I?" Words hurt to say when you have to tell your throat to speak them. Who could he even be speaking to? The trees waved against a tripping breeze.

You are in a place you were not before. You are here.

Tears had run thin lines against his cheeks. In a show of pride, he would not ask for help. No matter how small and sad his aloneness was, The Man could not bear the thought of trees beating him.

He swallowed his manifested understanding: had they truly left him? Was it his baffling inability or hubris? His emphatic trails of empathy? The Man growled, shaking such thoughts away.

He placed a bony hand on his face, trailed his fingers across sagging, bleached skin. Then, after forcing himself to imagine what he must look like, The Man decided to move the tendons of his legs.

Pop.

Yet another reminder of his fragility. But the tears were gone now, soaked into the ground beneath him and melted into the rivers upon his cheeks. The shaking came next, after a wave of nausea that sent him retching.

What will he do?

"Where did they go?" asked The Man, ignoring the scratch of his voice and wrapping his arms around his barren stomach.

Now they were silent.

"Where did they go?" he shouted, eyes glazing in memory at the tears he'd cried in his home of fire and rage. The snarls of his brethren upon finding him. Their eagerness in throwing him from the skies. He shook his head. "It was one mistake. One! Who am I if not—" The Man stopped. Who was he? Certainly they did not subject him to the cruel end that was mortality. Tears could not call for such a punishment.

There is no one else here. Was no one else. You are here, when before you were not.

The Man—after standing for such a brief time—fell to his knees, and snaking foliage slung from branch to branch above his hunched shoulders.

The growl of hunger was soon choked by his spine's scream. He stayed this way for a few more forgotten sunrises.

***

The clear starry night mocked The Man when he clenched his teeth and stood again, leaning a defeated hand upon a tree behind him. He had endured the same contemplation of forever, of dignity and tears. Caught in his self-centered revolution of misery.

The forest sniffed at his withering body.

He doesn't even know they left him.

The mention of being left—the sensation of abandonment—woke him.

Almost. He'd almost forgotten this. The Man turned, grasping the tree behind him, his hands like trembling moons. The forest voices hushed.

"Where am I?" he screamed, slamming fists against the bark.

He doesn't know that is not how trees feel pain.

"Stop it! Stop." He kicked the tree with his bare feet, the red of panic forgetting to tell The Man of toes and how they break.

The sickening sound of flesh on bark continued until the bloody pool of his feet could take no more, and The Man stumbled away from the spiderweb of vines and suffocating canopy of branches.

In his stupor, he staggered to a nearby clearing, the sky from which he was thrown melting into the horizon as grass climbed his legs. It seemed so easy to walk back into the stars. Instead, his knees buckled, pale hands raised above him. Reaching. His mouth hung open and silent. No words could excuse the tears streaming from his swollen eyes. The heave of his chest as he sobbed.

Yes, perhaps his greatest weakness: the trembling hope for love.

Oh, what it must be like, he wondered numbly.

The stars refused to answer, laughing and dancing in a world to which he once belonged. The Man lowered those hands to the dirt, dug the nubs of his fingers into the grass, and stood.

Looking down, he limped back into the forest.

***

The Man sat, legs crossed and palms open on the ground, eyes holding a drained, weary glare. Each blink trickled a hot sludge of humiliation.

Was it possible to give up without the necessity of purpose?

He hadn't given up, for sure, as tears still came no matter how much he wished for their dissipation. The Man refused to leave the canopy, unwilling to bear the stare of the conniving stars that teased his stretching fingers, that reminded him of the failures responsible for his exile into this wasteland of emotion.

The Man wept.

So pitiful. Ungodly. A shame to the forever in which he'd existed. The forest trees watched his aching contemplation.

Who are they?

The Man could hardly bring himself to remember anymore. It did not matter. All that he needed to know was that a place existed in the soft, blissful in-between of space and emotion, so much larger and unchanging in the arrogance of immortality.

But The Man's reverence could not bear silence. "They were tricksters, high atop imperious towers," he whispered. "They were caged to no world. No allies they bothered making." He gasped, eyes flying wide. "They are better than me in every way. They are the flames that bring life and the heat that melts it away. They have everything but the shackles of fear."

And The Man was one of them.

He now sat upon the dampened forest floor, glaring at trees, hoping it would break them. The spiderweb of vines still stretched above.

Now, how exactly did he leave such chains?

He is beginning to realize. To see.

His palms, scarred by earth's hot brand, closed. The carved rivers across his cheeks itched as The Man flicked away the constant drip of disdain and humiliation trailing down his neck.

It did not take much concentration.

No, The Man did not need anything more than a simple breath of thought. He stared at the grass and made it grow, their stems inching forward, stunned.

Oh, the forest voices were so silent now.

He basked in the sweet, chilling quiet and inhaled his foggy breath of control. Dragging his hands across the lengthened forest floor, The Man turned to a nearby bush. Made its thorns grow three times their size.

Glancing up, he stretched the branches above him so wide they blocked all touch of light. Darkness eclipsed him.

This felt so much better than the wallow of sadness. Now he turned toward a tree, one of the infinite many to mock him. Ignore him. Play with his mind and pity his circumstance. A sturdy, thick-rooted oak tree. The very one he'd beaten with weak limbs.

It was slow. Yes, The Man took his time forcing the tree's roots to slither through the softened ground toward yet another tree so ancient its bark mirrored stalled waves. He shivered in excitement, urging the root up into the air, where it wavered like a snake. The cool breeze hesitated as he sharpened the oak tree's end into a point.

He started low, near the Ancient One's stump. Twisted his fashioned drill of life until it broke into the bark's time-stamped waves. Silence spread as he pushed the oak tree up the trunk, grew gnarled roots until they spidered into the Ancient One's nest-sprouting branches. Twisted and twisted until the creaking scream of wood broke through the roar within his ears.

So The Man stopped, grasping the will of a third tree and forcing the Ancient One to crumble. That crash had no fight when it came to being heard. The web of vines tore and arched, sailing over The Man as he lay back, closing his eyes against a flaring ray of sun. He gnashed his teeth into a smile, again spreading leaves until nothing was left but pitch-black quiet.

He then dunked his head into whatever emotion this boiled-over thrill created.

There was no Time for guilt. No Time as The Man basked in darkness.

32

GONE

———

They left the dark, gratingly thick trees far behind them as grass, green and fresh, spread like moss throughout the forest. Nearly branchless trunks towered in the gaping forest spaces, and leafy-fingered ferns nestled beneath their sparse shadows. Sunlight, a contagious spark of brightness, spread around them.

"We're near the sun, I can tell," said Book, riding atop Time's shell, her grip tight as she gazed wondrously ahead. The warmed hands of summer had seemed to grab and stretch the forest by its ends.

"How?" asked Happy, walking beside her. The itching had returned, fervent and climbing along their scythe. They kept their gaze averted from Time and her splintered toes.

Book lifted a careful hand, pointing. "I can see it through the trees. The sun is too bright for even the forest to endure."

"I see it now," replied Happy, dragging their attention toward the leaf-tinged sky. The relieved trickle of what would be a smile. "I wonder what it will look like."

"Perhaps more beautiful than all the stars woven together," whispered Book.

Time, releasing a charcoal gasp, dropped to the ground.

A shining terror flashed across Book's shivering body as the frail tendon of balance threatened to snap. She steadied after a moment, nearly folded over, and her attention sharpened upon the wheezing, horribly exhausted tortoise, her wrinkled neck pulling for even a tease of oxygen.

Happy staggered back as the uncontrollable itching sensation slammed into their chest, beating with each fruitless tug. They searched Time's sunken, dull eyes for a glimpse of understanding. An acceptance of the approaching end. Book slid from the shell.

"Time, are you alright?" she asked, settling next to the ancient tortoise. She seemed hopeful, dreadfully unaware.

Happy laid eyes on the scythe protruding from their wrist, forcing it to remain by their side.

"No, Book. I am afraid not," whispered the tortoise, her voice clicking.

Afraid.

"I do think it will be over soon," she continued, looking up at Happy, her mouth open, shining with rot. "Please tell her, Happy. Tell her what you feel."

Happy forced the overwhelming instinct to falter, panic flaring. "But Time—"

"I am sorry you have no choice. That you have this burden."

Happy, burning with unkempt obligation, kneeled in front of Book, her brows lifting with a bleeding-heart kind of fear. "Happy, I know it is a bad thing," she said, tilting her head.

Happy wished to share her bubbling tears. To close their eyes and play at rest.

"Do you remember those voices that went away?" they said as Time wheezed through her green-stained mouth.

So quickly. She had seemed OK just yesterday.

"Yes. You said they were gone," Book replied, her voice chilling.

"They are. But these are separate feelings. I cannot ignore them."

"Why?"

"Because I must listen." Happy flinched at their own resignation.

"Is it like everything?" asked Book, eyes narrowing.

"No. I am not sure what it is other than inevitable."

"But you know other things now, Happy," Book insisted. "Can't you make them go away?"

"No, Book, I cannot," Happy managed as their scythe jerked forward. They dragged it back as Book's eyes widened. "It is unchangeable."

In a brief moment of comfort, Happy lifted a finger and touched a dark coil of her hair.

"Where will she go? How will we find her?" Book trained a hand to her rope, twisting it.

"I do not know, Book. I am so sorry." Guilt swarmed their pulsing eyes.

"Is it the After?" Book asked, desperate.

"Perhaps."

A panting, sunken breath turned their attention toward Time. The tug fastened itself to Happy's wrist. Pulled them forward.

"I must go," said Time, her head lifting from the ground. "I want this to end. Please, Happy, stop fighting."

"But we will not see you anymore," cried Book, watching as Happy was unwillingly dragged forward by the tether of their scythe.

"There is a price for the unknown," said Time.

Book clenched her powerless hands. "But I want you to stay."

"Oh, Book," said the tortoise, the warmth of fondness seeping into her words, "we are both aware of how little our wants affect the future."

"Don't go! We're so close, Time," cried Book, leaning her head against the deeply cracked shell.

The tortoise managed a rattling chuckle, her face gray and tired. "I am far older than you imagine. Please, understand that I am ready. I want to fight no more battles. I will be gone, but I am in no state to judge forever." She gave Happy a single nod. "Go on."

Happy glanced at Book as they keeled over in front of Time, their hands shaking.

It hurt to know she would never speak again. Her thoughts would be buried beneath the staggering fall of her lungs.

Happy begged guilt to subside. "Time, I am sorry. I am so sorry."

"You poor thing. Never apologize." She took her final breath and whispered, "You both have made my final days worth living. Thank you." She closed her eyes, let the flesh sink over them. Her head fell to the grass.

Happy dropped their gaze, Book's protests washing into static. They wished their arm would not lift. Wished the future would ignore them and turn away. They held a hand in front of their eyes, wishing they could close them.

Happy felt the barest touch of wrinkled skin.

The world turned white.

***

Happy stood in a world with no ground. No trees to avoid or dirt to walk upon. Nothing but a pure, still whiteness. In front of them sat a tortoise, deep green skin jostling as she looked up at them.

"Hello, Happy. I am sorry you think yourself so evil for doing what is right," she said, smiling.

"Time?" Happy replied, snapping their head to meet her twinkling gaze. "Time, I do not want you to leave. We need to find the sun."

Happy was aware that it was too late. There was no point in reversing what had already happened. They knew this was her soul, and how little weight a soul could bear.

"We both know I was never meant to finish such a journey," replied the tortoise, her wrinkles now complementing the soft rise of her mouth.

"But there is Book," insisted Happy. "She cannot walk."

"There are moments when strength finds us, though oftentimes it is at the end."

"Why must it be over?"

"Neither of us can answer that question."

But fear drove Happy forward. "Time, I am scared," they said, wrapping their lanky arms around themself.

Time chuckled, her tongue no longer crowded with fungus. "Of what, I do wonder?"

"I am scared The Man will come to find me," Happy explained. "That he will take me away from Book and our journey."

"Oh, Happy, I do not think he has ever had that power." When Happy did not respond, she continued, "The Man treads water, relishing the thought of drowning. He is a Man who hates that he walks across its surface."

Happy met her gaze. "I am not sure I understand."

"Happy, he looked beneath the ripples and saw you. If a Man can't become darkness, why not force it into the light? Crown himself king of the unreachable. You have nothing to break free from, unless you consider the imaginary."

Happy's gaze flickered to their scythe before they spoke, hoping the confusing jumble of their mind would later clear. "Thank you," they managed.

Time shuffled the restored freshness of her legs. "No, Happy," she answered. "Thank you. Thank you for being my friend." Her grin faltered for a moment. "Please tell Book goodbye for me."

Over.

That is all Happy could think as the shrewd canopy of reality breathed again. Soft grass beneath their webbed toes and distanced leaves shying from their kneeling frame. And . . .

A shell, just in front of their still reaching hand. Scarred by gaping cracks scratched by the seasons. Spiking and wide. And . . .

Empty.

Book solidified, her bleeding eyes lifting to meet golden lanterns.

Guilt—the harrowing chill of loss—crashed upon Happy like a weighted cloud.

"She is gone," said Book.

33

WHAT IS NEXT

———

She is gone.

Happy dropped to the ground, Book glancing between them and the empty space their scythe drew back from.

A soaking waterfall of anger cleaved into her stomach as the forest, lit by golden afternoon clouds, watched on.

"Book," whispered Happy, ripping their eyes from Time's shell and reaching out a hand.

She shook her head and turned away.

"No," she said, clenching her hands. Light warmed her unmoving toes. The roaring current forced through the collapsed tendons of her throat, burning her little mind. Oh, Time surely would not like Book to carry this horrid feeling of blame.

Happy drew their hand back, slouching upon the ground and tapping their fingers together.

"Time said—" they began, only for Book to snap her blunt teeth. Happy shrank back, shocked.

"No, Happy!" she shouted, reaching into the raging pool of denial. "Don't tell me what she said to *you*. You don't get to pretend now that I deserve an explanation."

"I thought you knew."

Flaming tongues of frustration. "How would I know it would be now?" she said, throwing her hands into the air. "How would I know I would be *left* here, Happy? You left me!"

Happy stared at her, their unblinking eyes utterly lost.

"Book, I had to. She was—"

"I know! There's the voices and The Man and some feeling I don't know about. So many things, and now she's gone." Steaming tears fell across her scrunched face.

"She was ready. She told us this, Book. Please, you are upset."

"Am I, Happy?" The shell pressed into Book's paling red jacket, craggy and jagged. Her poison words softened. "Where did she go?"

Happy dared a glance upward.

"I do not know," they said.

Book met lantern eyes. "Where did you go, then?"

"No place I can name. I wish it were easy to explain, Book. I am sorry."

"Another thing I don't know of," she managed through her frantic sobs. "She needs to be here. Bring her back, Happy. Bring her back like you did with me."

"I cannot do that, Book," Happy whispered, slouching their shoulders.

"Why not?"

"She is already gone."

Her swollen tongue sharpened. "And you took her!" She felt her words puncture Happy like a thorn. "So get her back!"

"Book . . ."

"I got nothing! I told her nothing. Gave her nothing to remember in the After she's gone off to."

Happy's eyes lit with a shivering hope. They tilted their pointed head. "But she told me of something, Book. She said—"

"I don't want to hear it."

"Why?"

She glared at Happy. "What words are meant for me if she wasn't bothered to use her lungs to speak them?"

Happy's eyes filled with pieced-together understanding. "You did not say goodbye," they said quietly.

The dried ends of her resolve turned ashen.

"I didn't get to have a goodbye!" Sickeningly, Book wondered if white flowers had meant anything to Happy. "She said things to you, didn't she?"

"Of course."

"But me"—Book's voice cracked—"I didn't even know it was today." She closed her eyes. "Happy, I didn't know I would have to remember her."

"We will remember together, then."

Book opened her eyes, the spark beneath them waning.

"No," she whispered, avoiding the exhausted tug of her emotions, "I think I want to be alone right now."

The silence was bitter, Time's shell void of the wise advice it once carried.

Happy dropped their head. "Do you want me to leave?" they asked, covering the tremble of their hands.

Happy her *friend*. The one who brought her back and left the pond for her and got sticks and loved her.

"Yes," she said, grabbing for her rope.

Book trained her gaze upon the frilled grasses before her as Happy stood, gazing at her with shaking, fearful eyes.

"I loved her too, Book," Happy murmured before turning away into the dusk-tinged forest.

Finally, the girl had chosen to be alone. What an empty triumph.

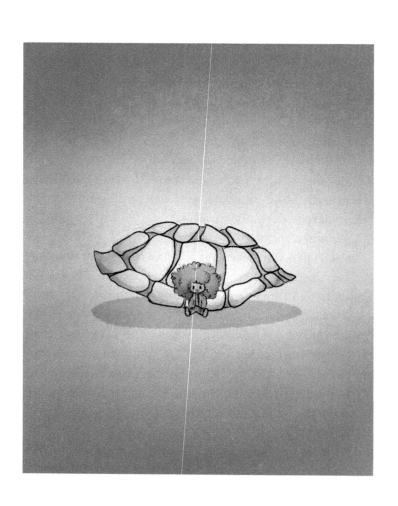

34

WHERE WE GO

———

Happy walked deep into nightfall, the pale-toothed moon lightening wide forest spaces. Their steps were slow and apprehensive as they kept moving, fearing the collapse that would come with stilled legs.

Time was gone. Happy took her. Of course they did. They had to. And now, Book . . .

Was that how friendships ended? Happy's webbed feet slowed, a pool of darkness in the silver night.

Was that how love goes away? Happy clenched their shaking hands, scythe curving toward the ground. How had they done so wrongly? What words could have kept the warming current of love in Book's mind? There was nothing to do, now. Happy stopped walking, choked on the thought.

Our friendship is over.

The poor being fell to their knees.

Oh, Time would not want Happy to carry such a horrid feeling of guilt. They folded themself upon the ground, their palms facing the clouded sky.

"I am sorry," they whispered, unsure who exactly they were apologizing to.

In one rise and fall of the sun, Happy had become completely alone. So close to the sun. No longer could they understand finding it without Book alongside them.

They remained silent, frantically unaware of what to do next.

Time was gone, and Happy's friend no longer wanted them.

Perhaps that is how love worked: a finite spin of luck. Ended by a blinking realization or the stalled beat of a heart.

An approaching pad of footsteps seized Happy's thoughts. Their golden eyes flickered with panic, staring fearfully into the grass.

"Why hello there," said The Man, stopping in front of Happy's outstretched hands.

Happy tensed the slouching bend of their spine as The Man crouched down, reaching with a finger to force their head up.

He smiled softly, almost sympathetic. "She is gone now, isn't she?"

"Yes," Happy said, drawing their hands back.

"Aw," The Man cooed, moving his palm to the side of Happy's head. "Are you sad, poor Creature?"

Happy dropped their eyes. Would Book care of The Man's presence? She lived in giant, engulfing waves of compassion. Surely she had not lost the boat upon which she sailed them.

But she wanted them to leave. Had drawn up the mast of her ship and thrown Happy overboard.

Rancid emotions soaked through Happy's mind, wrinkled skin etched into the smooth blankness of their scythe. Did Book ignore truth or simply defy it? A sore pull in their stomach told Happy thinking of a friend in such a way was wrong.

Was this the standard effect such loss caused? Being alone, and hoping for loneliness?

The Man's hand fell away as he stood, jerking Happy's head slightly.

"Now, you cannot stay on the ground forever," he said, grasping their arm. "Come now, do not let grief fool you."

Happy stood obediently. The Man stared at them, now gripping their shoulders.

"Tell me," he said, his gaze searching, "what has happened?"

"I—" Happy hesitated, tapping their stranded fingers. "Time is gone," they whispered finally.

"Yes, that is no surprise. But the *girl*. What of her?" The Man's eyes had widened, almost excited.

"She asked me to leave."

The Man loosened his grip, stepping back. He brought a hand to the trailing scars along his eyes. "What did you do?"

"Time had to leave," Happy insisted, growing desperate. "She was ready."

"Ah, yes, but tell me," The Man said, smiling, "there must be more."

Was it so terrible, to wish for affection?

Surely a gentle touch carries no venom.

"I am lonely," Happy said, forcing their words and sinking beneath bloodshot eyes. "This today is so different from what I thought it would be."

The Man gave an unsurprised sigh, his skin ghostly. "They have truly broken you," he said, looking behind Happy into the wide forest beyond. He beckoned them forward. "Come now, you have had your fun. Let's get you back."

Happy looked down, aching and empty. Caught between the tethers of longing and frustration. The Man grasped their hand and tugged them into walking.

"Come now," he repeated with an edged gentleness.

Happy dropped their head and followed.

***

Book cried alone, Time's shell an eerie press against her back. She was sickened by her want to push it away.

"Help," she whispered to the night creatures trilling high above. They leaned toward her, chirping warily, their prying eyes carrying not the current of pity, but confusion.

Why had she pushed them away?

Book twisted the rope between her fingers, unable to answer.

Her flaming, tear-stained anger had collapsed into raw exhaustion. She picked at the remnants of her flared emotions, willing them to tell her why, but they were dampened and limp.

A fearful gag clawed up her throat. The morning would come with no voice but hers.

Book rested a trembling hand upon Time's shell, running her thumb across its swirling cracks.

She was gone.

Book forced herself to recognize that Time did not leave by choice. The bitter truth of endings must be swallowed, willfully or not.

Happy was her friend. That was enough. Had always been enough.

Chirping crickets began a riotous tune.

She pushed them away.

"I know!" Book shouted to the no one around her. She pushed her legs, willing them to bend. They, of course, remained still.

As night continued on, Book twisted her head frantically, searching for golden eyes tucked between leaning forest trees.

Perhaps Happy had not gone far. Perhaps they decided not to leave. To ignore her wishes.

She wrenched at the rope, heated anger slashing into her neck with a raging arc of flame. She let out a frustrated groan, chained upon the ground.

Happy had always listened. Taken her words and sailed them across the golden waters of their eyes. Never were they one to understand betrayal.

She slumped against Time's shell, trying to remember how many wrinkles had existed on the sloped rise of her neck. Book thought of her words and the sunrises she'd spent loathing them.

And she thought of a long-ago when Book and Happy had sung a song and told stories. When their worries flowed between them in a washing shore of understanding.

She peered again into the lightly shadowed forest, desperate for the friend she'd thrown away.

After again finding nothing but mere branches, she turned back to Time's shell, pressed her cheek against it, and closed her eyes.

The forest was silent as Book pretended to dream. Without breath, she soon became frustrated at her own inaction and popped open her gaze.

And with a flooding jolt as if woken from a nightmare, Book remembered him. The lightning-strike realization of The Man who had tried so ardently to take Happy away. And she, Happy's friend, had just nearly wished for that to happen.

Book jerked up, turning to the rocky, boulder-like shell for a whispering moment.

"Goodbye, Time," she said, wiping her trailing tears away. "I'll get Happy back, and we'll find the sun."

She drew her fingers away, training clouded eyes upon a distant clump of trees where she'd last spotted the sullen tread of Happy's feet.

Ignoring the trembling grasses beneath her, Book lifted an arm and dragged herself forward.

***

The Man swept a hand before him, talking incessantly with a triumphant tinge to his otherwise dry voice.

"I must do so much to right this imbalance," he said, glancing furtively toward the dark sky. "You have not been gone long enough for them to notice, I think."

Thinly spiked vines still slithered along his ankles as they walked through the forest. A soaking confusion nearly bent Happy in half. Often, their webbed footsteps halted, only for a sharp yank of The Man's pale arm to make them stumble.

Again Happy faltered and was dragged onward.

"What are you doing?" The Man demanded, turning the scarred mess of his face, patience washed from the sharp clip of his words. "They are gone. You should celebrate! Cheer in the hopes we may revive everything." Another tepid glance above.

Happy's fingers were limp in The Man's solid grip. "She said she loved me," they whispered quietly, looking at the grass squashed beneath their webbed toes.

The Man scoffed. "Do not be fooled by baseless emotions. Temporary words."

"She told me it was an *always* feeling."

"Yet here you are, wished away. So easily called upon and cast aside," he said, touching his tear-stained cheeks. "Love is useless, do you hear me? An utter waste of memory."

"But—" *How do you know of love?*

He wrenched Happy forward.

"Look how wretched you've become," The Man almost shouted. "Look how beaten. Pitiful."

Happy fell silent.

"And me," The Man continued, eyes glazing, "I have been there for you, always. I did not have love to confuse me. I did not need love to tell me to care for you. I have been here, reaching for you even when I was so harshly shoved away."

"But did you?" asked Happy quietly.

"What?" The Man stopped walking.

"Did you care for me?"

The Man released a short burst of laughter so unlike Time's gravelly chuckle.

"Who is holding your hand, poor Creature?" he said, squeezing tendrilled fingers. "Who is rescuing you from the hole you've found yourself in? You are lost, indeed. Your finicky emotions have utterly cleaned you of hope." The Man scraped his eyes across Happy's frame. "Do not pretend my words have suddenly lost their meaning. I created you. Molded your skin. Care is whatever I deem it."

The night held its breath, shielding the approaching dawn.

"Then," Happy began, "Where is your love?"

The Man snarled. His airy victory snapped beneath flashing teeth.

"Have I not just answered that ridiculous question? Love is but a word—a manufactured emotion destined for regret."

Time's words flashed before Happy's rusted gaze.

Who are you at your barest? An existence. An undeniable piece of everything.

They suddenly wished to pull their hand away. Straightening their slumped shoulders, Happy whispered, "I do not regret my love."

The Man's throat bobbed. "You will."

Happy remained stubborn. "But I do not."

"Foolish, insolent Creature!" he shouted, his words falling dully upon the thin trees around them. "Are you incapable of learning? I know your empty mind. I created it!"

"If anything," Happy said, "it seems you carry regret in the space love should be."

Finally they'd glimpsed the bare, pulsing flesh of The Man's words and, with a bubbling spout of confidence, Happy tore their hand free and spun around, striding back the way they'd come. The Man did not follow.

As morning peeked from some distant horizon, Happy suddenly realized they did not know who they were headed toward.

Their strength evaporated, and they sat upon the soft, budding grass. Perhaps The Man was right—they were empty.

***

A faltering light peppered the ground before Book's trembling fingers, each lift of an elbow followed by a knotted crack of her bones. The aching drag of her body carved a matted trail, trees towering above her.

She sucked back misery and stuffed it into the numb chambers of her feet. Ignored the gutted emptiness of leaving Time's shell behind.

Guilt both pulled her forward and dragged her down, willing Book to atone for the act of giving up.

Suddenly, her jacket snagged on an edged rock and a brushstroke of panic seized her constricting neck as her slow travels halted. She raised an arm, pulled against the immense weight of her little body, and collapsed forward, her nose pressing into the soft grass.

The tears again came, for just a moment.

She turned her head, scooping up the crumbs of her will-power as dew soaked through her jeans. Gulping a useless breath, Book forced her elbows to bend in a staggering pop. Forest creatures silenced their morning cries at the pulsing echo. She continued moving.

As the sun finished its rise, Book tried the aching threads of her voice, reaching toward her friend in the dismal hope they'd accept her apology.

***

A soft, tepid shout touched their senses. "Happy?"

Their head shot up, and Happy's lantern gaze darted through the scattered forest trees. A checkered light spotted the grass.

"Happy?" she called again.

Stumbling to a stand, they fell forward, arms waving like a black-hole beacon. After a brief hesitation, they answered.

"Hello?"

Gasping cries of relief led them to their friend.

35

GRIEF

———

They spent many sunrises upon the ground, Book stuttering through conversations and gulping apologies.

The absence of leathered words and breathing lungs tinged the breezeless air.

A midday light broke across the forest as Happy held a pebble within their slender hand, perhaps imagining it as a shell.

"Happy?" Book whispered, clutching at her rope.

They dropped the rock and looked to her. "Yes, Book?"

She pushed tentatively against the tense wall between them. "What are you feeling right now?"

Happy glanced down. "I feel heavy," they said. "As if all of those things I knew were not going to happen are upset I hoped for them so much. As if the clouds have turned to stone."

Book nodded. "Me too."

"When he came for me," Happy continued, and Book's jaw tightened, "I do not think I have ever felt so hopeless."

She swallowed another apology, knowing Happy found it exhausting to accept so many.

"I know," she said simply. Pale hands and empty shells.

A brief smoke of silence.

"Would you like to know," Happy said quietly, "what she wanted me to tell you?"

Book grasped desperately at the extended olive branch, shamed by her past actions.

"I would," she choked.

"She wanted to say goodbye."

Book sniffled.

"I didn't know it was so simple," she managed.

Happy shrugged. "I do not think there was much else to say beyond that."

"But I didn't get to tell her, Happy." Book met their lantern eyes, allowing the biting sadness to climb toward her stalled heart.

"Tell her what?" Happy asked, leaning forward.

"That I love her. I never told her."

With a faint rustle, Happy reached for a coiled strand of Book's hair, dust clearing as vulnerabilities bared themselves.

"Do you know what she said to me," Book continued, voice trembling, "when you went looking for sticks alone?"

"What?"

"That pasts are forgotten, presents are ignored, and futures are foggy with sleep. But you and I don't sleep, Happy," she said, the taste of loss bitter on the swollen gag of her tongue. "Why can't we see the future if we cannot dream?"

"I do not think anyone is meant to know what will happen," Happy replied, meeting her scrunched gaze. "Even things that do not live. We are given only the inevitable, distorted ends."

Perhaps the tears weren't done with her. "Foggy blurs and shapes did not tell me it would hurt this bad. And the past . . ."

"What about it?" asked Happy, their voice gentle.

"I keep thinking about all those nights I spent wishing she would leave us. I would whisper it over and over in my head, Happy, up and down with the sun. I wanted my legs to work so that she might go," Book whispered, clutching at her rope. "How many stories have we missed, simply because I wouldn't listen?"

Happy paused, golden eyes steeped in all those ideas left now to memory. "It is the past," they whispered to her. "Her stories have been lived through and must now be remembered. Of all the misshapen futures, this one is clear." As if flinching at their own incentives, Happy drew their hand back. "I do not think we were to know," they finished.

"To know *what*?" asked Book, wiping quiet tears away.

"To know how greatly we would think of pasts and futures. How badly it would tire our eyes."

Book's molten emotions welded themselves into a gleaming sword, dragging their pointed edge across her memories until a single, glaring arch of iron sliced through rippling skin and wise voices.

"I think I know what we are feeling, Book," Happy said, hesitating. "The Man told me of it."

She lifted her slumped head. "And what is that?"

Happy met her bleeding eyes. "Grief."

Book drummed her fingers together as the sword lodged beneath her chest. "I do not much like that word," she whispered.

But lingering grief stayed with them, hollowing a place where Time once lived and nestling into the folds of those lost things that are forever wished for.

***

The girl and being sat together with this shell for many more days, drifting in and out of futures and pasts, speaking to one another with the kind of utterly lost voices that are painful to listen to.

Yet, as will all things, Time must move forward, and a morning finally rose when Book looked at her friend and lifted her purple lips into a smile.

Once the two friends could speak the word "remember" without regret or heaviness and with only the somber acceptance of the irreversible past, Book and Happy lifted the soggy ends of their spirits and carried onward.

Book, without much strength in the remnant frills of her legs, continued dragging herself along the bouncing forest floor, lifting her arms in stuttering bursts of willpower.

After three more sunrises, however, even the determined ends of her fingers could offer no more.

36

STUCK

———

The forest transformed into a shifting mass of dribbling, pebbled sand. Fronded palms looped arms with oak trees while clouded light illuminated a million different pathways like toothy gaps. Book and Happy inched forward, clumped parcels of grass eyeing them warily as a pulsing heat danced through the forest.

Book's jacket, once cherry red, now held within its torn stitches a washed, exhausted gray. Adventure's sponge had scrubbed it loose of color, but hardly did she mind, as even the sky never once held a rainbow. If anything, Book's jacket now mirrored the puffy clouds above, bringing her closer to the stars.

How funny now, for each drag of her arm slowed the sun's approach, its home teasing them with each bright flare of dusk. As afternoon sauntered forward, tugging away the sheeted light, Book's arms finally sputtered and stalled. Her fists opened with nothing but sand within them.

"Book?" said Happy, their webbed feet beside her. Crouching down, they peered at Book and her worn jacket. "Why have you stopped?"

"I don't think my arms can take any more, Happy. They are not like legs," Book bent her elbows, pushing against her bones until they relented with a *pop*, sinking her rope-leaden shoulders until she could prop her head and meet Happy's lantern gaze. "I don't know what to do," she admitted.

Book wondered if this was how Time felt, her determination overcome by the suddenness of bodies and how quickly they mold. Her little memory flinched.

"Maybe they will work in the morning, once we have let them rest," said Happy, settling upon the ground, a leaning palm tree behind them. "Time said strength will find you, as we are almost at the end."

"The end?" Book cocked her head.

"The end of our adventure."

"What if it's like last time, Happy?" Book said, dunked in the cold water of dread. "Where we continued forward only by luck and Time? What if we don't make it?"

Happy turned their lantern eyes to the misted sky. "It is different now."

"How?"

"Because we have changed too much," Happy said. "We are different than we were before. Maybe it is a simple solution, or maybe it will be more difficult."

Book chuckled, hesitant worry shaking her laughter. "You have traded my *what-ifs* for *maybes*," she said.

Happy met her gaze. "A maybe sounds better than a what-if, don't you think?"

Her warm smile trickled. "I do think so." After a moment, she noticed Happy cautiously searching the sandy forest behind her.

"What are you looking for?" asked Book. She tapped her fingers along the ground.

"He has not yet called for me," they said, dropping their golden stare. "I am worried he is coming soon."

"Maybe he won't."

"What if he does?"

"Then," said Book, running a hand upon the pebbly ground, "I trust you enough to do what is right, even if it may seem like the wrong thing." Her smile was eclipsed in guilt. "I have certainly done wrong things with no belief in their imaginary goodness. But I know you, Happy. Sometimes, I think you are made of goodness completely."

Happy mirrored the gentle brush of her fingers. "I like knowing I have made mistakes," they said, "I feel more real that way."

Book's smile brightened. "Of course."

"But," Happy continued, "I am afraid he will hurt me."

"Oh, Happy, I am sorry," Book murmured, clenching a fist into the sand.

"But I am the one who has left so many times," Happy insisted. "Who has followed the sunset flowers." The forest creaked around them. Dusk settled upon splayed tree branches above.

"And I sent you to him," Book said, her voice certain. "We are both mistake makers. And anyway"—she batted at the dangling end of her rope—"I finally understand I should not be upset with you, but with The Man I've never met."

The battling confliction of agreement and defense shimmered across her friend's golden eyes.

"He is troubled," Happy whispered.

"Yes, I know."

They waited until darkness overwhelmed them.

***

In the deep pit of midnight, Happy shot up.

Arms. If nothing, The Man had arms.

"Book," they whispered, squeezing the pebbled ground.

She peeked through her hair. "Yes, Happy?"

"He can help us."

Book's gaze flew open against the swell of her cheeks. "What?" she asked, blinking.

"The Man," they said, the idea sputtering and desperate. "He has hands. He has arms, Book. Arms and hands and a body that moves when he tells it to."

"He is not like Time," Book replied, pushing a gentle hand against Happy's sparking enthusiasm. "He doesn't want to help us. To dirty his hands with sympathy."

"But I can ask him. I can ask him, Book. It will be simple. A single question."

"You have never received an answer before."

"But it is only one. One question that needs one answer. I can do that. We must reach the sun. We cannot wait for the seasons to take us." Happy looked down at the scythe curling out from their wrist, remembering The Man's fingers upon it. "I have learned so much. I have been apart from him long enough."

Book flinched. Guilt crawled into her frown. "But he almost got you."

"We were apart then."

"I know," she murmured, "and I am sorry. Every day I am sorry."

Happy grasped a curl of Book's hair.

"And every day I will forgive you."

Book grinned with teary relief, smoothing her twitching hands.

"And if he says no?" she asked, her smile wavering.

"Then we will find another way. It is too close, Book," Happy insisted, drawing their hand back. "I do not want this to be taken from you." They looked again at their scythe, Book following their sullen gaze.

The curving limb ate the moonlight, surrounding itself in a cloudy fuzz of darkness. Her face twisted in a brief moment of contemplation, as though wondering what The Man had possibly done to her friend.

How terribly selfish to hurt that which knows not what pain is.

She tugged a faint hand at the end of her rope, looking back to Happy. "OK," she whispered.

Happy lifted their pointed head. "Thank you," they said, shoulders slumping with relief. The ground shifted as Happy stood, night skies glinting through the wide-fingered trees above.

Book closed her eyes as a scarlet flower bloomed beside her. She did not see Happy observe its twirling dance. Did not see those golden eyes narrow.

"I love you, Book," Happy said. "I will be back soon."

She nodded. "I love you too, Happy."

And they sank into the brush, becoming yet another lanky trunk among the shadows. The flowers sprouted and tickled their webbed toes.

***

She waited until Happy's crunching footsteps pattered into nothingness. Until the flaming petals beside her withered beneath the ground. Then Book, finding the strength memory's voices promised, crawled after them.

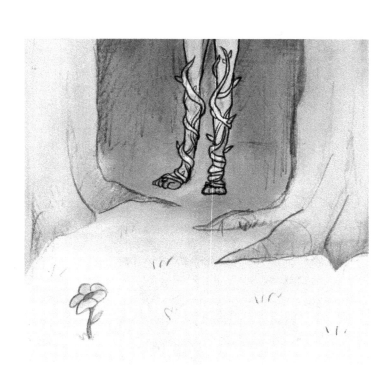

37

THE MEETING

———

The scarlet pathway had just shriveled away as The Man, flanked by two sickened oak trees, stood at its sanded end. Spiking vines climbed his legs like green cogs, grinding into the rusted metal of his skin. Happy stilled their nervous feet and straightened the curved slouch of their back.

It was only one question.

They cast an unfocused gaze forward and tripped into their words with a floundering determination. "My friend cannot walk," Happy said, snipping the edges of their syllables. "We are so near the end of our journey, but her legs do not bend or move."

The Man tilted his chin, smiling. Tragedy stained him horribly, his arms beaten raw in the savage hope the skin might open. "So you've wounded my intentions only to come crawling back," he replied, lurching forward and grabbing for Happy's scythe. As they snatched their hand away, The Man bubbled with laughter.

"No, it is not so simple." Happy's voice was stone, and The Man fell silent.

"You have one of them leave you," The Man said, waving his empty fingers, "and another who is so near ending. Now tell me, poor Creature, what have you done in both these aching situations?"

Happy did not allow themself to step back.

"You came to me," The Man said, his teeth glinting. "Here still I stand, and you are without her. Your little carrier has left you."

They thought of their friend, of decisions, and the number of wrong ones they believed to be right.

"No," Happy repeated.

The Man raised a hand, ticking his fingers in front of the narrowed furrow of his brow. He glanced at the scythe extending from Happy's wrist. "That so?" he whispered.

"I cannot say where she has gone, but I will not accept even the thought that Time abandoned us."

"You are mad," The Man said, glaring at Happy, "to believe yourself capable of defining the end."

"I do not want even to understand it." Happy clasped their hands, straining to keep in sight the stagnancy of bloated feet. "Everything," they said before falling silent.

The Man dropped his hands, that horrid smile flipping into a snarl. "What of it?" he snapped.

"You told me I was to know everything. You said it was infinite in its complexities, full of light and darkness and burdening your shoulders with its care." Happy's voice turned sour. "But you lied. You lied to me about everything."

That snarl frothed. "Stop it!"

"You said many things, and I now wonder if any of them were true. The mistakes. The punishments you forced me through." Happy dared a step forward, confidence a budding stem in their chest.

The vines along The Man's legs fell and dug themselves into the sand. He soon followed, a collapsed waste upon the sparse forest floor.

"Why?" Happy asked.

He turned his pale face away. "You would never understand," The Man whispered.

"No," Happy agreed, "I do not think I would."

The Man hates his shame, hates the way it tears through him.

"There are stories," they continued. "Stories that fit everything into the folds of their lessons."

"So *everything* is an easy solution, while the end is nothing but a questioned myth?" The Man was overcome by his anger, gasping. He looked up from his crumpled position on the ground.

"I see everything," replied Happy, hardly meeting the fury-dazed glare. "I see it in the stories I speak. In the skies that hold them."

The Man heaved his frail bags of human lungs, back arching against a pressure of his own narcissistic making. As Happy watched him, a peachy whisper of memory came to them.

Time crept through with her long, wrinkled neck.

"Before is nothing but a memory," she murmured from the clouds Happy imagined her to live in. They swallowed the solidity of her assurance.

"Everything is beyond us," Happy said, taking another step against dripping fear, "but please help us. We are so close to the sun."

The Man slouched farther, silent.

"It is so close, perhaps not even a night away," they continued. "But she cannot walk. And I cannot carry her."

Tears pierced his eyes, flooded the carved rivers along his cheeks.

"Please." Happy dropped their radiant golden eyes. "Help us."

The Man's voice came soft. A caress of sound. "Never," he said, as if his red mouth were poisoned.

And there, deep in Happy's midnight stomach, the leak of fear ignited into white flames of hatred, sharpening their gaze with the sweet fire of loathing. "You have taken so much!" They shivered within burning claws, crushed by the delicious hope of pain. "You never tell me why, for I do not think even you can face it. I was your toy! A game!" They jabbed their scythe toward The Man who craned his head, eyes frozen wide. "You will not do the same to her! For once! For once, you will give."

Happy stumbled back at the realization of pointed fingers. The jarring terror of anger smothered the smoking embers in their stomach, and they dropped their arms.

The Man said nothing, his pupils pooling in the sagging shores of his face as he stared past Happy.

Before shame could capture them, Happy turned around.

"Book?" they said, the shock of yelling coursing through them in a beating wave.

But she too was not looking at her friend. Her bleeding gaze, just above the forest floor, fell upon The Man who cried behind them. She averted her stare and blinked the swells of her eyes. Hushed her tears.

Oh, dread was a horrible emotion, and it curled around the little dead girl's heart.

"You," she breathed as The Man crawled back.

The sinking weight of realization.

"I know you," she said, touching her rope's frayed end.

"Hello, child," The Man whispered.

Again that burning, immortal fury swelled as Book's tiny body racked itself in sobs.

"No," she screamed, but her throat long ago lost the ability to feel itself ripping, "you took that from me!"

The Man opened and closed his mouth, searching the decayed ends of his brain.

"It was far bigger than—"

But the girl screamed as her eyes glazed in memory.

Happy knelt beside her, caught in the vise of panic. At their helpless, slender fingers.

The Man staggered to his feet, vines returning in a menacing flash. He wiped at thin tears as vulnerability grabbed for his toes. Snatching his feet away, he tripped back into the forest, his footsteps trailed by a dense air of regret.

"Book," said Happy, reaching for her coiled, trembling hair, "I am so sorry."

Take, take, take.

The dead girl cried, clawing at the rope around her neck.

38

THE LITTLE GIRL

An Autumn Not-So-Long-Ago:

What is a sunrise if your eyes are closed?

It is still blindingly bright, of course. Harsh and bleeding. The Man did not much like blood. Did not like the way forest beasts sniffed and washed themselves in it. Did not like how the tang of fear lingered within thick, inky streams. Yes, blood was messy and lasting. Gushing even after pulses ebbed or eyes dulled. How many bodies did he step on simply by walking?

This ground is flavored with carcasses. Disgusting.

Still he wandered through the forest, thickening grass beneath his toes with a twitched finger. An autumn beam of sunshine flashed into his eyes, and he forced the golden leaves above to widen, throwing light back into the sky. His frown, carved within the cracked stone of his lips, remained taut as he continued in darkness, striking matches of self-loathing against the dry wood of his mind.

Have them stutter at my anger rather than laugh at my tears.

Yes, he truly believed the skies watched him. As if now, after a million lifetimes, they were finally compelled to look. Foolish Man.

He had to do just one thing.

One thing is so far less than any other number. Shadows lengthened with sunrise's curtained light, fading into a myth of beauty and beginnings.

He did not notice an overextended tree limb scream just behind him. Did not hear as tendons snapped, ripping loose until the sky was blocked no longer and the legend of light basked in a momentary sigh of reality. But The Man did not notice, for trees do not bleed. The growing fire in his brain melted his feelings, slipping past the clenched rungs of his fingers.

I know there is something. There is something.

He continued away from the pond, where the Creature twiddled its spiderlike fingers, staring with incredulous, stupid eyes.

If only he could love the Creature. Offer It something to know of and cherish.

A betrayed piece of his soul wanted to turn back, though, and he hated himself for it. The grass around him sagged as he shook the confused strands of his mind, willing his thoughts to turn. Perhaps he could block those gills slashed upon the Creature's skin. Bury It beneath sopping pond water. He smiled quietly, and grass sprung forward in life.

But it was not Time for the Creature and the little games they played together. Another fallen branch, another broken cry.

It is Time for something to happen.

The Man walked until his burden grew legs and stepped with him. Until the callousness of his threats made shadowed flowers bloom, enclosing him within a dark tunnel spotted by petaled stars.

His gaze froze like ice at a sudden plop of water. A bright flash of fabricated red.

Why couldn't she have seen him first and run away on bare feet?

Because she is a child, you fool. She is a child, and children are not to be plagued with such responsibility.

Here the sun shone in tepid brushes, shimmering within a creek's glassy ripples. And there, balancing upon watered stones, was a girl. Her coiled, dark chocolate hair bounced as she jumped from rock to rock, nearly falling as an emerald dragonfly zipped above. Her dark-skinned hands poked out from puffed jacket cuffs, stuttering laughter cheering the thickened forest trees.

The little girl smiled as cool mud squelched between her toes. The Man's frown deepened into a line of contemplation.

His leggy burden grew arms and tapped his shoulder. He shrugged, nearly turning back. Nearly stamping out the fire, the pain, the everything. He was unfixable. Then the burden sprouted hands and held his head still. Because—really—it was just one thing. How horrible could it be if he did just one thing? Make them see him. Make them revere him. Take him back.

The girl now sat, ogling a bunny not ten feet from her. She did not appear lost, the trees cradling her dreamy smile and pockmarked jeans. Her innocence made him angry. The anger convinced him of intention. A breeze ruffled the girl's hair as she studied a fallen leaf, oblivious and naive.

The Man opened his hands, willing a flower to take shape within the slender bend of his palms. Its petals folded in perfect scarlet symmetry, bowing to golden whiskers of pollen dipped in a charred black center. Pausing for only a moment, he crushed it within his fists and dropped it to the ground.

The forest looked away from coiled hair, suddenly choking on the flower's bleeding, crumpled body. But The Man didn't much like blood, and refused to imagine the stains on his fingertips as anything more than something.

No, he thought, his plan laying itself before him. He would not crouch and hide from this child. He was proud. *I am proud and strong, and she is weak. Stupid, weak, and frail.*

Slowly, red flowers emerged like a glowing trail. The girl stared wide-eyed at a set of blooming petals across from her.

The Man watched on, standing tall behind an oak tree.

Without even hesitating—she still smelled of curiosity and the future—the little girl jumped to her muddy feet and skipped across the water. Nearly slipping, she crouched down, running a hand over the silken bloom.

Perhaps she wouldn't pick it up.

Then that hand rested beneath the flower as if holding a glass, and she plucked it from the ground. The forest averted their eyes and the bunny scampered away.

She looked up to find another flower, centered around fallen leaves in a bright splatter. Again the girl followed, smiling as she plucked this one as well.

Another.

Another.

Another.

The child was so happy, blissfully unaware of the someone walking behind her, posture straight and skin poisoned. They continued this contradiction of life—a girl chasing beauty grown from the tentacled beast compressed into a human behind her—until a pond opened before them.

She carried now an armful of vibrant, identical flowers, her hair a curled wreath as she gazed at the pond, trees dutifully bowing toward its lapping shores. Smiling, she wondered if perhaps she had found a secret hiding spot. A place where her fantasies could be reenacted. Where she could be a queen, a pirate, an explorer, a god.

The Man stepped out from the trees, and she dropped her flowers.

"Hello, child," he said, careful to hide his teeth.

She examined the reddened bundle upon the ground. "Hello," she mumbled back.

"Do you know who I am?"

"No," the girl responded, finally meeting his curled gaze. "Do I need to?"

"Of course not. Those are lovely flowers you have there."

She smiled. The damned child *smiled*.

"Thank you! They led me here." She beamed, hardly noticing The Man's scarred eyes.

"Yes, it does appear that way," he said, taking a quiet step forward. "Doesn't it?"

Jolting with a sudden realization, the girl lowered her voice to a whisper. "Did you see me with the flowers? Are you looking for a secret hiding place too?"

"Oh, no, I am not. I'd be holding the flowers if I were."

The Man grinned with the sharpened ends of his teeth. A sudden, spilling dread filled the shocked tremble of the girl's eyes. She swallowed her breath and fell silent.

He strode forward with feigned confidence, close enough to spot the dried mud upon her toes. Setting a palm before her quivering gaze, The Man grew a silken red flower, forcing its petals to twirl and dance.

Vines, leathery and thick, snuck up the girls pockmarked jeans. Her lips wobbled. *Only a child.*

The Man examined the flower in his hand, turning it over in search of any blemishes that might distinguish it from those on the ground. Green tethers hung now from the girl's arms. Shadows traced along her skin. The pond did not once ripple.

"Where is my family?" she managed through the gagging panic in her throat.

The Man dropped the flower and looked away. Something, something, something. A tendril reached, covering her mouth and those large, innocent eyes sprang loose with tears. She didn't struggle as this feeling no child should feel blackened her heart and hopes. He walked away to a nearby tree, its bark a sagging brown. With battling hesitation, he pulled a rope from a hole dug at the divergence of two mottled branches. Held it between his hands.

"Oh, don't you see, child?" he murmured, turning back to her. "This is the only way to fix all that is broken." He again approached, gently wrapping the rope around her neck. "The only way. There is too much for me to explain, but I want you to know one thing." His words were near pleading. "Nothing will follow this. It is simply over, and you will be gone."

She gasped and tried sobbing, but the forest held her still. The Man focused upon a lengthy knot he was cinching to her neck. The girl closed her eyes, but the pull of her straining neck forced her to open them again. *Only a child.*

He drew a hand back, wiping at her stream of tears and flicking them to the ground. A few paces from them sat a lone willow tree, darkened trunk growing grudgingly upward. Its weeping branches swept toward tangled forest grasses. Behind the girl, so she could pretend a little longer. Because in stories, little girls got saved or broke free. But little girls didn't usually have ropes around their necks.

He picked up the crying, scared child, and carried her to the tree, ignoring the brush of her hair. She could not struggle as the grappled vines clung to her.

The willow shivered as The Man stood beneath its weeping canopy, setting the girl down and grabbing her chin.

"Why do you cry?" he whispered. "You have nothing to fear. All that would have happened is over. Just a few moments more, child. Just a few more moments, and you will not have to worry anymore. Nothing is far more preferable to possibility."

He sighed at her sniffled response, tying yet another knot at the end of the rope to slip through a naked branch of the ancient willow. Without notice, the vines had slunk away, draining beneath the little girl's still muddy feet. Her flickering eyes were forced to watch, unused to the suffocating weight in her chest. In reaching an end she did not yet understand.

The last face she'd ever see was a stranger with pointed teeth.

With his gentle hands, The Man lifted her into the air and onto the branch. A soft creak of wood.

It took longer than he'd expected.

He did not look away.

And when she stopped shaking, when he was sure her bulging eyes held no light, The Man turned to a now pitch-black sky.

"Look at my hands," he shouted, voice cracking. "Do you see them shake? No. No, for though you've choked me dry of immortality's blissful numbness, I did the same to her. To a nameless girl. I've lived in swooning mountains of emotion but have not even begun to climb toward its peak."

Then he broke away with a betrayed sob. The girl's limp body was unmoving, as the breeze no longer dared touch her. He cried in front of the ripple-less pond, lips filmy with saliva. And when he turned away, he cried in front of the flowers, wilted upon the ground. Falling to his knees, he tore them apart, ripping each petal until a bloody massacre lay before him.

A glimpse of dangling toes had him running, until the moonless night sent him collapsing within the shallow creek. Soaking, he got up and ran again. The forest didn't bother to stop him.

Only a child.

39

A BAD CONVERSATION

———

Happy's unblinking eyes drooled a pressing confusion into their curled fingers as they grasped at coiled black hair. The Man's fleeing rush echoed throughout the hesitant dawn. Book had gone still, her mouth open as memories funneled through her.

"Book," Happy whispered, leaning toward her, "are you alright?"

Take, take, take.

The mantra chanted and swung within their thoughts.

"Please, Happy." She gasped suddenly, a desperate strain to her voice. "Please understand—" She glanced at them feebly, sunken upon her sandy elbows.

Still playing the song of ignorance, Happy glanced back at indented footprints slashed into the ground. "I do not know why he left," they said, again turning to Book, whose legs were splayed behind her. "I am sorry. I can feel that something bad is about to happen, and it hurts to speak through."

"There was a before," Book managed, jerking her head up. "A Time I existed, and a Time stolen from me. That is why he left you, Happy."

Happy drew their hands slowly away. "But Time is gone," they insisted. "Time is gone and told us *before* is only a memory."

"I don't have even a recollection of before," cried Book, her voice sputtering. "I wasn't spared that! *Before* matters if it's forgotten!"

The melancholic whistle of truth played.

"I am not sure I understand," Happy murmured, dropping their head.

Book sniffed, gazing at the fronded trees around them. "I am not living," she said.

"Yes, I know that."

Tears now glistened in her bulging eyes as Book spoke past her swollen neck, the rope almost swallowed by decay.

"Happy, please listen to me. I *was*, though. I was living."

Almost automatically, Happy responded, "But The Man says—"

"It was him, Happy," Book interrupted. "He did this to me."

"But I brought you back."

"He is the reason you found me."

Happy leaned back, clutching their legs. "Then why is that a bad thing?" they asked quietly.

Book shrugged, stilling the tremble of her lips. "Because I never should've been there."

"But then we would not be friends," Happy said. "We would be strangers without love."

"But Happy, there were people," Book insisted, pleading with rounded eyes. "Other people who loved me."

Happy shook their head. "Yes, but they were living."

"*I* was living!"

Silent, as jealousy sharpened her desperate tongue.

"Happy, listen to me," she said in a dejected whisper. "We said the flowers are what a sunrise ought to be. But I know them now. Happy, I *know* them. Please, that is not a sunrise, but blood."

Happy wanted to understand. It hurt them to feel this. To feel lost.

Without a sincere embrace of sympathy, Book dislodged her withheld tears.

"Book, I want to help you," said Happy, an icy pour washing over their golden eyes. "I do not like seeing you cry. Please do not be upset." Frantic, they reached for her coiled hair, only to snatch away their hand upon seeing the glinted end of the scythe.

"It is the flowers," Book said, hardly meeting Happy's fearful gaze. "The Man and the flowers have made my legs fail. The rope"—she did not bother touching it anymore—"he placed around my neck."

Happy got to their knees. Too many bad thoughts in their friend's words. A weight so deep in the sag of her eyes.

"Why did you meet him?" she asked, the dangerously simple question cowing her fluffed hair.

Happy watched their feet sift beneath the pebbled sand. "I wanted him to help us. To carry you," they said, stabbed by the branding heat of shame. How foolish now, to believe The Man capable of goodness.

"But what did he tell you, Happy?" she said, calming her sniffled words. "What did he say all those sunrises ago when we first started our adventure?"

"He told me"—oh, how much Happy wished they could cry—"to leave you. To go back."

Book nodded. "And what did he say after Time left and I sent you away?" she said, voice quivering.

"That your love had ended. To go back," they repeated.

"Did you ever think of listening?"

"Only once," Happy whispered, forcing their shaking hands to still.

Trust was the only strand keeping them together. After a stilled breath, Book spoke again, her expression open and unsurprised. She furrowed her brows, looking to Happy.

"And what did he do to you? When you would not listen?" she asked.

A barrage of memories flitted through Happy's mind.

"Nothing worth mentioning," they said, hunching their shoulders.

Book untied the fickle strings of Happy's lie. "Tell me," she said, "has this rope been used for more than a chain around my neck?"

A dark, patient moment, like the air after glass shatters. "Yes."

"Oh, Happy." Still Book cried, but no longer for herself.

The forest was silent but for the little dead girl's sobs. The girl who had once been like them.

After a while, Happy again touched the frayed ends of her hair.

"I am sorry," they whispered.

A tear dragged across the pockmarked swells of her cheek. "You have done nothing wrong," she said.

"I left you. It was a bad thing to do."

She looked at her hands buried in the sand. "I pushed you away," she said. "That's a blame only I can take credit for."

"Book?"

Their eyes met.

"Yes, Happy?"

"I need to speak to him one last time."

She blinked. "Why?"

"Because I have questions," Happy said, glancing at their scythe, "and I want them answered before we finish our journey."

"What will you do with these answers?" she asked, a fading afternoon light tossing gold spatters across her hair.

"I will keep them. Use them to understand and learn."

"Okay." Book offered an exhausted smile, rustling the rope cinched to her neck. "I believe you."

Happy stood, melting into the fast-approaching darkness. They met the swollen pupils of Book's gaze.

"And Book?" they said.

She pushed her head up. "Yes?"

"I never wanted to leave. Please do not think I ever have."

"I know," she said, again smiling.

"I will be back."

Happy turned and followed the rushed, sandy footprints. Leaning branches managed to hide their lanky frame.

Book rested her head upon the ground, dreaming of a family she could not remember. The forest watched her, imagining the breath she once held, and, for a moment, finally carried the weight of guilt.

She was only a child.

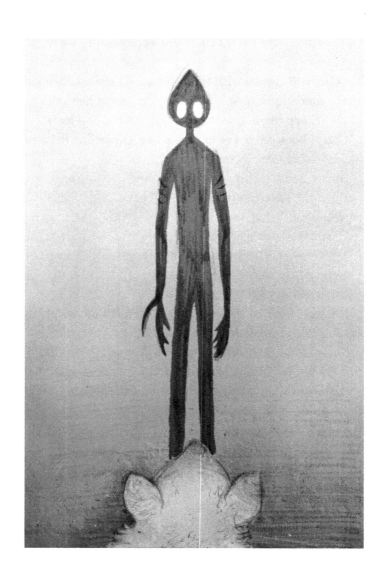

40

BLINDED CREATURE

———

Book had disappeared in the sparse forest brush when Happy found The Man, collapsed upon a slim sandy clearing and flanked by two trees like broken wings. He raised his scarred eyes to meet Happy's lantern stare, his shield of false arrogance wiped from his face in the darkness. So unlike the millions of memories Happy was forced to bear. The forest shrank back, with fronded leaves straining toward the sky and gnarled bushes hiding the delicate tremble of their flowers. The Man, in the center of it all, appeared small as he wept.

Happy couldn't help but think of their friend not so far away, also trapped upon the ground. She too held tears. But Happy could feel the palpable beat of their differences. Book was a small thing, but never by choice.

The Man wanted this, Happy knew. Realizing such a sad, bleeding truth was horrible. They buried the sizzling embers of anger, wishing them to never again light.

The Man smacked his lips together, shoulders heaving. "Do you remember what I told you?" he gasped. "Of the place I am from?" His spine shuddered when Happy didn't respond. "They hated me there," he continued, choking on the wallowed trill of his sobs. "They threw me into this disgusting, wretched world! My tears compelled them. My *compassion.*

I wanted to get back, you see. I had to get back! I tried. Oh, I tried so hard to feel their rage. Recreate it in my corrupt, sad little mind."

Happy did not move, their arms flattened to their sides. "I do not remember you being sad," they responded bluntly.

This earned a cough from The Man, his pointed teeth flashing. "Of course you don't," he said, and spat on the ground. "You were never meant to remember anything beyond that damned pond. If I could have just kept you there, maybe . . ." His face contorted with a denied realization, voice dropping to a whisper. ". . . but I did. I kept you there for so long. And no . . . no, I don't think they noticed." He was no longer speaking to Happy but mumbling to himself in a desperate, stuttered sort of way.

"When did you come from the other place?" Happy asked, remembering tender hands and a rolling sunset. It was all they needed. An answer, an explanation. Something to help this wrenching dread. Book was alone.

The Man's scowl was so insincere in its harshness, he looked almost comical. "How long do you think I have been here?" he said.

Happy shifted their feet. "Longer than I have."

"Yes, but not by much."

"You created me."

"I did," The Man said, pressing his palms against his eyes. "I did because, unfortunately, flowers and trees offer me only so much entertainment."

"Why me?" Happy said quietly, stepping forward. They thrust their scythe in the air between them. "Why am I here?"

"Oh, you poor thing," he said, sighing. "I could ask the same question of myself. I guess we are both trapped here, aren't we? I can hardly remember the other place. Only that I once lived there and that its surface was made of fire."

Silence beat its lifeless wings, clouds heavy and dark above.

"Your friend," he stammered through those cavernous tears, "I did not know her before . . ."

"Before you took her too soon," Happy said, eyes burning with the flashing image of a rope, a birch sapling, and the constant gasp as trees watched their child fall and crumble before the bark had even hardened.

The Man clutched his sides. "When I"—he waved a hand—"I thought perhaps they'd take me back. If I just showed them what I could do."

"But she is a child. You did nothing but take a child," said Happy. It hurt to feel such putrid anger. To hope the whip of The Man's actions would tear across his skin. "How have you so idealized a place no longer existing in your memory?" they asked, clenching their hands and willing such pain away.

"You must understand how much bigger everything is than this little copse of woods you've traveled through," he replied, still folded upon the sand.

"I cannot know of everything's size, but I know it is far larger than whatever you plan on using it for."

"Why would I—"

"It is sad you believe yourself so powerful," Happy said and looked back toward where they'd come. "That you think yourself greater than these trees. Nothing should ever tell you to do such a thing."

The Man shook his head. "I am not horrible," he whispered.

"Then say my name," said Happy as The Man pressed himself into the ground, mouth closed as to keep the strangling grasp on his own guilt. He blinked, and a tear dribbled down his scarred cheeks.

"You know I can't do that," he managed to say.

Happy's hands fell again to their sides, their voice suddenly pleading. "But why must I believe it?"

"Because this has never been about *you*. You were never to exist beyond my grasp. To have a name. Yet here I am, on the ground, with you above me."

Happy's glowing eyes held a pitiful glare. "I do not need to listen to a Man who cannot even say a name," they said. "You imagine a directionless land to somehow have you at its center."

"Tell the girl that I—" The Man said and gnashed his teeth, let them cut through his trembling lips, "—I did not wish to hurt her."

Happy nearly walked away. Their gaze hardened.

"Then what did you wish to do?" they asked.

"I wanted only to leave," he said, closing his eyes.

"And you believe that is enough for my friend? I have seen you use a rope. I have felt it on my wrists. So, please, do not tell me you 'did not wish.'"

"The world is cruel to me," The Man pleaded, his breaths frantic.

"How long have you been saying that to believe it so fully?"

"I'm—" But he couldn't finish such futile words, his throat bobbing. His eyes flushed wide before sliding into a half-lidded gleam of submission. He ducked into the vacuum of his crouched self—shrinking, shrinking, shrinking as brown fur rippled across his skin like dirtied water. A long, leathery tail sprouted around his rapidly shrinking body as the sounds of his deteriorating self overwhelmed his choking breath.

A stuttered crunch followed the rippling tremors of The Man's body as his human bones jerked and folded in half. His limbs turned to small, hairless paws and a wet crack dribbled from his covered mouth. Lifting his head, he revealed a horribly wrinkled snout, pointed teeth forcing the jaw into a constant snarl. His ears curled outward, large and obscured by ragged mats of fur.

And his eyes. It took Happy a step forward to realize that the creature had none. In their place were two long, oozing seams of purple skin.

The creature, sensing Happy's shadow, looked up, its tail flinching.

They stared at each other for a long moment, Happy's orbed eyes meeting empty sockets. It could not see them. Could not see how Happy's hands shook.

The creature was blind.

It squealed at the darkness its ruddy body wasn't used to and turned around, scurrying beneath the sand and scarce trees.

Stunned, Happy watched it disappear, waiting until the forest again went silent. They gazed at the barren ground, alone and without sinister voices to tell them they were dreaming.

A frog's distant chortle came, the apprehensive rustle of tree branches, yet still Happy remained, the moonless night offering no shadows.

The Man, in all his lifetimes and words, could not accept the one truth of mistakes.

41

HAPPY'S BITTER SADNESS

———

Alone.

Too many swirling, fragmented thoughts lodged themselves into Happy's tortured brain as they stood alone in the clearing, sand bubbling beneath their feet.

"Where?" Happy whispered before falling to their knees.

Surely, human hands and scarred eyes could not simply fade away. Turn into a scramble of fur and mange. It couldn't possibly be that simple. Happy knew this. Of course they knew the complexities of endings.

But that was no ending. It was so different from the way Time had drifted and left them. Happy searched the ground for purple, empty sockets. He hadn't reached the end.

So where had he gone?

The fragments glowed with heat. Burned like fire. Happy held their sides, screams of betrayal and utter loss ripping through them.

How? How could they feel this way?

They stood, looking manically toward the sparse tree branches. Their footsteps were short and quick, from trunk to trunk. A drawling heat thickened the otherwise dry night air.

Happy had not loved him. No possibility of such pining love existed. No chance it slumped unconsciously upon Happy's shoulders for so long. They'd never wanted it.

But what of the past things? Where had the pity come from?

Is it love if you've been tricked into it?

Happy rocked at the end of a severed rope, leaning over the cavern of their abuse. A deep, pounding voice echoed the word *why*.

They stood, creeping through the sanded forest, desperate to find the ragged creature and pull The Man from it. It wasn't fair. It wasn't right for Happy and their poor friend to face all he ran from. *Runs* from, for wasn't he still scurrying on tiny paws?

Happy stopped, staring down at their own webbed toes.

And if they found him, what would they do? Questions—the important kinds—never received an answer. And Happy couldn't cry. Couldn't show The Man how horribly they felt inside.

Happy again fell to the shifting ground, head sinking between spindled shoulders.

How much had been wasted for the simple hope of reciprocation? A delicate hand? A kind word?

Too much. Always too much for The Man to offer glimpses of genuine care.

Oh, what to feel in the exhausted battle of emotions? The war of memories callously squashed Happy's foolish hope.

Foolish, The Man had called them with his working mouth. It seemed he had been right.

A numbed shock rippled across Happy's spine at the realization that The Man would never speak again. Again, because he was still here, for such a Man—who can touch a scythe without fear—does not reach endings.

Happy swept his eyes over the curving extension now, twisting it like a shadow. Ghostly fingers suddenly skimmed across its surface, and Happy flitted their pulsing gaze away.

They had tried. Every day inside the pond, Happy had *tried* to understand him. Had revered the feet they believed walked for the sake of everything, The Man's shoulders slouched by an infinite weight. Happy was told to follow, hold up their arms, and lighten such a responsibility.

Happy gripped their head, slowing the rushing storm of guilt-ridden thoughts. How were they to know that *everything* was an uncontrollable, storytelling fantasy? How were they to lessen The Man's tailor-made burden? How were they to do anything at all before carrying a name?

"A lie is hard to spot if that is all you are ever told," Book had said to them not so long ago, her true words sizzling beneath Happy's sunken frame. Again they pulled at their legs and stood, lifted by the strings of her soft-spoken honesty.

Perhaps it was not understanding. Perhaps Happy, too, was blinded. Sight muddled by pond water and The Man's gaze. They began walking toward their friend.

At least with Book, they knew it to be love. True and kind and terrifying love.

They ducked beneath a splayed group of branches, finally realizing that a beginning filled with decay and strangled necks was not one to be desired. A forest's flinching disdain was never asked for.

The Man had burdened Happy with a coal-stained memory and torn Book from her living life. Happy swallowed this thick pill of truth. Forced it down their breathless throat.

They walked onward, wishing for coiled hair and wise words. For knowledge that would stay with them forever. No longer was there a voice to contradict it.

***

Happy rounded a thick-trunked, mottled oak tree and spied a dirty red jacket just ahead. They rushed to Book, falling to the ground and cradling their head.

Her hands, wringing themselves upon her lap, jerked forward. She had managed to crawl toward a bending palm tree, leaning her little body against it. The forest seemed too dismayed by their own actions to be fearful. Too ashamed by the little girl who should be walking.

"He is gone," said Happy, shaking.

The tension of life and befores without rope or decay laid itself between them.

Book widened the bleeding pupils of her eyes, silent.

"Book?" Happy whispered, looking to her.

Her fluffed hair was a black moon in the pale night, waning as she tilted her head. "Yes, Happy?"

"Why do I feel grief? Why is it inside me?" they asked, clutching their chest.

"I don't know," she said, appearing surprised at Happy's sudden debilitation. "I wish I could explain so many things."

"I did not listen to you," Happy said quietly. "I chose to believe his words."

"This is not your fault, Happy."

"He has ruined me."

"No!" Book shouted, bracing against her arms and jolting forward. "You freed yourself from him. Don't get sucked into a past you have severed yourself from."

"But it lives within my memories. Always."

Her words almost hissed with insistence. "Perhaps," she said, "but do not forget your name."

"My name?" Happy said and took their hands from their face.

"Yes," Book said, "your name. It is a wonderful name. And I gave it to you. You are Happy, and The Man never could take that from you. Do you want to know why?"

"Why?" Happy sat up, meeting the beaming intention of Book's gaze.

"Because, Happy, you left the pond. You left the pond and started an adventure," Book said, waving a hand between them. "You followed the red flowers and came back. He took things from you"—she paused for a brief, ticking moment—"and me. But we kept walking. And when we couldn't anymore, Time helped us. And when she had to leave, we crawled."

"But he came back," Happy said quietly.

"He did, and still you returned to me! Even when I sent you to him, you trusted me!"

A glowing, rayed hand reached toward Happy as they hung over the abyss of their thoughts.

"I am so tired," they whispered, fighting the slouch of their shoulders.

"I know. But I will be with you. I will not leave," Book said and offered a tear-stained smile. "Even if my legs worked, I would not leave." Sand dripped from her hands as she clasped them together. "And you won't ever leave me."

"Not ever," said Happy, nodding. They looked above, to the sky of stories and everything. "I do not know if I miss him or if I miss what was never offered to me."

"Perhaps it's like the family from my living life," said Book.

Happy's golden eyes widened. "What do you mean?" they asked.

"I miss so terribly what I never had," she said, twiddling her fingers. "It lives inside of me now, all those maybes. But I am not sad." She wiped her muddy face. "No, I don't think it's sadness, but a melancholic kind of wonder. An ache for memories I should know."

Happy quirked their head, imagining a past if The Man hadn't carried such sharp teeth. The cool river of longing.

"I think you are right," they said.

Book sighed. "And Happy?" she murmured, her voice gentle.

"Yes?"

"It is almost over."

Happy turned back to her. "I know."

"I think we will find the sun," she said. "Tomorrow."

A curious fear.

"The end," Book continued, lying down and spreading her arms wide. "Do you think I will make it?"

"Time said you would," Happy replied, following Book and resting upon the sand.

The two friends fell quiet as night sailed through the depthless sky, a pale darkness settling across wide forest leaves.

Happy let The Man's washing tide of words push and pull in their memory. Pain was constant, but tonight they simply let it slide across them and into the obscured stars.

42

UNWANTED

———

Stars.

So many of them fizzing above the watery clouds.

It did not feel like when last she'd seen them. As if the millions of millions of other worlds were somehow immune to pain.

Did not bother with loneliness.

Which star had The Man come from? Was it even a star? Perhaps he'd fallen from the entire sky, dipping out of a reality unseen by Book's blinking eyes. Eyes that should have remained open until the forest things turned her into dirt and mud.

She released an airless sigh with Happy silent next to her.

He was not scary looking.

Book could hardly remember the sharp edges of his actions, caught in blurred touches and an understanding that she used to be someone else. A someone who breathed and lived and knew other breathing things that did not want her gone. Loved her.

She'd never believed she could be anything other than herself. Never asked why she carried a rope necklace. Never recognized the dotted connection between life and death.

"I am not supposed to be here," she whispered suddenly, breaking the ice of her thinking.

Golden eyes met her own.

"Then where else would you be?" Happy asked. Their voice trembled with the guilt of confusion.

"I do not know," Book said, turning back to the night sky, "but before I was here and after I was living, there was supposed to be something. Something different than this."

"Book, I do not think—"

"It is the After that Time told us of. I was to go to the After." She waited a moment, testing the words in her mind. "But you brought me to this. To this in-between."

Happy said nothing.

"I've always known this, Happy. Of course I have," she continued, eyes trained toward the wincing stars. "And I would never want to go anywhere you are not. But"—those golden eyes waited as Book lit up with the frail spark of realization—"I did not know it was an accident."

Happy did not look away.

"That you did not want me." Tears filled her eyes.

Book wondered if the stars ever looked at The Man and all the things he'd done.

Or was that it? Was that why he created Happy, simply because they wouldn't spare him a glance?

"That could never be true," Happy replied.

The Man was gone, no matter how the stars acted.

"Do you mean you did it on purpose?" she asked, tugging at the dirtied zipper of her jacket.

"No, because I had never done it before," Happy said and sat up, hands folded in their lap. "Because The Man never said I could do such a thing. Book, I did not mean to do it, I cannot even imagine tricking you into such a lie. I made what I was told was a mistake. But then you blinked and spoke to me and answered my questions." Happy, too, looked to the stars. "You are so much more than whatever lessons The Man taught me. More than whatever idea made my intentions an accident."

Book sniffed. Wiped her tears away.

"I was awake," she said, as that was the only way she could now think of describing it, "before I met you, Happy."

Their shoulders slouched as Happy tilted their head. "Were you?"

"Yes. When my eyes first opened. Or"—she thought for a moment—"when they opened for their second first, I was alone. Is that why you weren't there? Because you didn't want to face me?"

"Not at all," Happy interjected. "It was the voice. It ripped at my mind, berating me for such curiosity." They gazed at their scythe. "Hardly did I believe anything would happen."

She puffed a half-hearted laugh. "Never would I blame you," Book assured her friend.

Happy gazed now at the breezeless forest around them.

"What was it like, being lonely?" they asked.

Book quieted. "I could ask you the same question," she said.

"But I have only just begun experiencing it, Book."

She dropped her hands to the ground. "Why?"

"Because," said Happy, searching for words, "I did not know loneliness was a feeling I could indulge in. No friend made my aloneness turn sour. And"—Happy wiggled their fingers limply—"he was always there, watching me. That is not what I would call loneliness."

"Yes, I think you're right," Book said, furrowing her brow. "Perhaps that is how I should have known I was living."

Happy looked at her.

"What do you mean?"

"I felt so"—Book cracked open her memories—"torn away. I wanted a presence that met my gaze or filled a gap I figured the forest had ripped in me. Perhaps that is what makes someone living. They taste loneliness without even knowing."

"But I am not living, Book," replied Happy, grasping her explanation, "and I have certainly felt such a way after meeting you."

She smiled. "Maybe we haven't been describing life correctly."

The forest inhaled her little words, rustling collectively.

"Sometimes," Book continued, her grin fading, "I think my soul is made of dust."

Happy stiffened. "Why is that?"

"I am not sure. But when we find the sun, I worry it will all disappear. That I will go with nothing left inside of me."

A breath.

"Book," said Happy, reaching for her hair.

"Yes, Happy?"

"I have been here longer than even Time, and I have touched many things those ancient feelings told me were ready to go. I could feel them leave, and not one left without their soul."

She blinked her bleeding eyes. "Are you sure?"

"I have never been so certain." A moment of decision. "When I touched you, I felt your soul."

Book's smile reignited and she reached a hand above her. "And what did it feel like?"

"Like when horrible tragedies strike down forests, and they manage to rise again."

Book sighed, waving to the stars.

"Thank you," she whispered.

43

BOOK STANDING

"Book?"

The dawn light poked at the girl's wavering thoughts. "Yes, Happy?" she said, lying flat upon the rugged sack of her jacket, swollen eyelids pushing into her watery vision.

Happy rustled beside her, sand rippling across their midnight skin and filling the forest with a gentle *shhh*.

The sun was so close now, as if it were real. A yellow splotch of tangibility.

"Are you ready to go?" Happy asked.

Book struggled to sit up, resting a shoulder against the tree behind her. "Do you remember our song?" she asked, smiling.

Her friend tilted those golden eyes. "Of course."

We travel the forest trees.

Book leaned forward, testing the stability of her arms. "Remember how I said you can say words that mean something different?"

"Yes."

"Well," said Book, almost shy, "when we sang in the rain, I didn't change any of my thoughts. My words were exactly how I meant them." She looked past the sandy forest, where the sun would eventually rest its sleepy, rayed eyes. Slowly, she rocked to her side, pulling at her legs like stones.

"I did the same," replied Happy, grasping a tripping curl of Book's hair as she fell back.

We make choices and choose right.

They sat together, content in the in-between as sluggish heat pulled at the wide-fronded leaves above. After a long, yawning moment, Book pressed at her nagging curiosity.

"Where did he go?" she asked as Happy's tendrilled hands receded. Again, she leaned forward, forcing her toes to wiggle.

We feel good things and no fright.

They gazed at her, drawing circles in the sand. "I am not sure," they said.

Book quirked her head. "What do you mean?"

Happy shrugged. "I think he wanted for too long. He made hate where there was none, placed fear where it shouldn't be. He tried so hard to be something bad. And," they said, their circles turning into a mass of spirals connected by swooping curves, "I do not think he could ever bring himself to accept it."

"Do you think he feels the longing for a family, too?" asked Book, finding within her still heart the stain of understanding. She had just managed to lift herself from the ground before sand shifted her arms and she tripped back into the tree behind her.

Happy met her eyes, cautious. "Perhaps," they said. "He became a creature, Book. No bigger than my hand."

"He did?" she said, halting her incessant attempts at standing and widening her soft gaze.

"Yes. He curved his back until it shrank and grew fur. The . . . last Time he looked at me, he looked at me without seeing. He can never again find us, for he has no eyes to find us with."

"And our journey is almost over," Book murmured, wiping her hands.

Happy stilled their circle-drawing fingers. "Yes."

What will happen then?

"Do you miss her?" asked Book suddenly, flexing her feet in the growing humidity.

"I do," Happy said, looking at the bleary sky. "I miss her every day."

"Me too." Tears were a sudden crowd upon her eyes. She blinked them away. "Sometimes," she continued, "I think memory can be a good thing, even if it hurts a bit." Book smiled glumly. "It's how we see her, before the future sweeps us away."

Happy wiped their sand painting back into smooth blankness. They stood.

"This has felt quite like a dream, hasn't it?" she finished.

"What has?" Happy asked, gazing at their scythe.

"Looking for the sun. And dreams can't live for long."

"That is true," Happy said, peering through Book's hair. "You are wise, Book, but your appearance tells me that now."

Book picked at the rusted zipper of her jacket. "Why now?"

"Maybe because now that I know you, you look a little different." They turned back to the sky, those lantern eyes following the inevitable. "Or maybe going to a new place has changed you."

Book grinned. "But I've changed in a good way?"

"Of course."

Book, too, looked above, her dusty soul humming with the pang of endings. For once, her mind did not quiver with fear, lulled by a dreamy stillness. A calming warmth of withheld wonder finally flowed through the current-less pump of her veins. As she dropped her gaze to the shifting ground her feet would soon step across, a breathy flash of green twisted at the edge of her vision. She spun toward the bite of color.

An emerald dragonfly whizzed and zipped in the heated air, beating angelic, paper wings as it dipped into a brief, elegant bow. Its blurred form flew into the sparse forest and toward the sunrise.

Her legs tingled.

"That's nice," Book said faintly. "Thank you, Happy."

***

As the little girl struggled to a stand, her friend remained near, wrapped in apprehension. She tugged at her last threads of strength and pulled herself up as a gentle, cheek-kissing breeze came. Her fluffed, coiled hair embraced the pale wind that had fled so long ago, and she held her hands out wide, smiling.

Her friend beamed, shaking themself from the fringed cuffs of worry.

The two turned to the sandy, nearly treeless landscape, a wavering heat skipping along the pebbled ground.

The girl swung a leg forward.

Slowly, just as they did at the journey's twinkling beginning, they began walking side-by-side.

No scarlet red flowers or carved stone shells led their way.

Me and you and I.

44

THE BIG POND

Hours and hours they walked, Book tottering next to Happy as the pebbled sand climbed their ankles and trees slunk behind them. The stripped, yellow tinged forest now extended infinitely in one shifting upward slant, quiet but for the sodden crunch of footsteps. Sometimes they talked, and sometimes their heads were filled with silence, the end so near it pulled at their fingers.

Deep into afternoon's shadow, they waded up a sloping hill, heat draining beneath their feet as they reached its crest. Slowly, the two faltered, eyes alight as before them lay a brilliant red sky, dancing across the horizon with a swooping flare of clouds. Book began to cry.

"It's a sunset, Happy."

Happy did not respond, as The Man had given them that much. Their steps were short as before them arose a grand pond, so large it was beyond imagination. Waves rippled until they touched the sky, swathed in depthless eternity. And there, painting one final picture before treading darkness, was the sun.

Happy, without inhaling the poison of what-ifs, blinked their giant golden eyes, trembling as the fiery landscape sank into orange and red. Then to purple. Then to the deepest black.

They looked at Book, a leftover pink just touching her cheeks. She smiled with a sadness so simply beautiful and treacherously knowing, the sun hesitated in its departure. Contemplated a world without endings.

Still the darkness came, cradling them in its sleepy arms. And though Happy could not smile, they felt exactly what it must be like to have a sad one. They felt the icy pour of love.

"Book," they said. "I must go into the pond." A brush of her coiled hair.

She met their pulsing gaze. "Is it the ancient feelings telling you to?"

"No, it is not. Book, you must understand," Happy whispered, hesitating. "We have finished our journey." Slowly, Happy felt their long-cradled purpose unfurl into the dark waters before them.

A small tear fell down her cheek. "Of course I do, Happy. We found the sun," Book replied, sniffing. "What do you think is beyond a sunset?"

"I am not sure. Perhaps it is the end." White-ruffled waves lapped at their toes, urging them forward.

"Then," said Book, looking down, "I must go with you."

Happy memorized the dipping lines of Book's face. "But it is over."

"This adventure is," she agreed, flexing her fingers as if remembering she was human, "but infinity is in everything. We could find another story."

A calming assurance washed across what Happy believed to be their soul. "OK," they said, gazing out across the enormous pond before taking a small step forward, Book beside them.

As the water reached their friend's knees, Happy grasped her hand, their scythe curving between them. The calming darkness hushed their fears.

"I love you, Book," Happy whispered as they continued, wishing for Book's final words to be lovely ones. "Are you not afraid?"

Their footsteps were washed clean from the sand.

"No, I don't think I am," she replied, her hair dusted with sprayed droplets. "Finally, it is just me, you and I, and the sun."

Love no longer seemed as complicated as Happy had imagined. They walked beneath the now ripple-less waves.

ACKNOWLEDGMENTS

We made it, folks! Draft after draft after draft, and here we are!

In terms of thank-yous, I first want to thank my mom and dad for investing in my future and encouraging my dreams. I know it can be a rarity to have such loving parents, and I am grateful every day for you guys.

Thank you to all the editors I've come across, including Michael Bailey and Jessica Drake-Thomas. You handled the wide-eyed ignorance of my questions and helped mold me into a full-fledged author!

To my illustrator and friend, Elizabeth Chong, *wow*! Let's all give a round of applause to those absolutely stunning illustrations. You depicted my story in such a beautiful way and actively took time out of your school life to help me. Thank you!

Thank you to my grandparents, who bought enough copies to give to all my twice-removed cousins.

To those of you who preordered my novel—and thus helped finance its entire publication—I thank you. I was simply stunned to watch the mass of people come to help me—from soccer coaches to friends, schoolteachers to bosses, mentors to neighbors. Thank you for believing in me and giving my story a home. I truly was not expecting so much love.

Mia Macias, Chris Palmer, Chelsea Carwile, Madison Sudekum, Brett Krueger, Teresa Trumble Guerrero, Vuong Prieto, Monse Dohogne, Shannon Hofmann, Elizabeth Chong, Eva Khattab, Aryn Bagley, Anne Clark, Kimberly Foust, Leah Osborne, Kathy Cody, Daniel Norton, Asas Husain, Michaila Spradlin, Maria Perales, Heather Smith, Brooke Mckinney, Sabrina Jordan, Pam Branch, Maria Berry-Marhsall, Uncle Tom, Sara Rimann, Stacy Hosford, Sherry Donahe, Sarah Janosek, Rachale Franklin, Doug Chasteen, Doylene Oxford (Nana), Julie Sawaya, Haytham Najjar, Mark Andersen, Rob Cheshire, Robert Long, Michelle Atherden, Manuel Hernandez, Michelle Bell, Chastidy Vernengo, Lori Truslow, Leane Crowther, Laura Coleman, Laura Richardson, Kelly Aaron, Eric Koester, Janis Hoge, Laylia Hairell, Anna Costarides, Jacqueline Messer, Kendal James, Erik Huddleston, Debra Radomski, Raul Anand, Carla Coursey, Clayton Gush, Isabella Jaimez, Uncle Ricky, Bianca Sanchez, LaKissa Bright, Ashley Madison, Amanda Scott, Sara Hesskew, Coach Bauer, Nana Taylor, Jaiden Dennis, Abigail Perea, Wendi Nitschmann, Albert Csaszar, Antonio Paredes, Kristen Holladay, Karen Alexander, Aunt Debi, Jennifer Dutton, Coach Munger, and Amy Steindorff—thank you, thank you, thank you!